there you are

there you are

a novel

JOANNE TAYLOR

Tundra Books

Published in Canada by Tundra Books,
481 University Avenue, Toronto, Ontario M5G 2E9

Published in the United States by Tundra Books of Northern New York,
P.O. Box 1030, Plattsburgh, New York 12901

Library of Congress Control Number: 2003112017

National Library of Canada Cataloguing in Publication

Taylor, Joanne
    There you are / Joanne Taylor.

ISBN 0-88776-658-7

    I. Title.

PS8589.A895T46 2004   JC813'.6   C2003-905207-9

We acknowledge the financial support of the Government of
Canada through the Book Publishing Industry Development
Program (BPIDP) and that of the Government of Ontario through
the Ontario Media Development Corporation's Ontario Book
Initiative. We further acknowledge the support of the Canada
Council for the Arts and the Ontario Arts Council for our publish-
ing program.

Design: Terri Nimmo

Printed and bound in Canada

1 2 3 4 5 6   09 08 07 06 05 04

To my sister Jeannie, who said, "Why don't you write?"

Margaree Valley, Cape Breton

• •

It was Jeannie Shaw's favorite time of year but, after what happened the September she turned twelve, those last weeks of summer always held a flash of sadness, like one red tree warning of winter along a green hill.

The day before school started, Jeannie was blueberry picking alone. The hill meadow rippled with heat. She wiped an arm across her forehead. "It's too hot for September!" she protested. She tugged her cotton dress away from her legs and returned to filling the old shortening pails.

Berry season had lingered on, like the hot weather, this year. The wild blueberries were small and grew on low bushes. It took a long time to pick carefully – no stems, no leaves, no pale pink or hard white berries. Mrs. Campbell, at the store, said Jeannie was the cleanest picker in the valley. Jeannie would sell one pailful to Campbell's Store for twenty-five cents, and Mama would be waiting for the other. Jeannie tightened her ribbon to keep her damp hair in place and got back to work.

So hot! It was the first of September, but it felt like July and August put together. No rain softened the air, or slaked the dust from the wild rosebushes beside the roads. All the men listened to the radio for forest-fire warnings. All the women used well water sparingly. And everyone was careful with lanterns and matches.

When she'd filled the pails, Jeannie turned to catch the breeze. She looked out over the Margaree Valley, with its winding silver river. Fold after paler fold of forested hill-side hazed into the distance. Mama always said, "There may be places in the world as nice as this, but there's nowhere nicer."

Jeannie could see a few chimneys, a few roof corners among the trees. Thirteen families lived on this stretch of the river now. Their community was growing at last. She wished for one girl her age in any of those homes, but there wasn't such a girl in the whole valley. Not one. When school started tomorrow, the same handful of students would sit down in the senior classroom, but only she and two boys would actually be in Grade Seven.

The boys weren't worth bothering about, she'd decided on her very first day of school, and she hadn't changed her mind in the years since. Boys never cared for anything but hunting and fishing and horsing around. She'd tried to be friends with the three older girls in Senior Room, but they acted as if she didn't exist. Those girls – always giggling, always posing as if they thought they were in one of those movies at the theater far off in the city, turning their backs when Jeannie came near. In her mind, she called them the Three-Headed Monster of the Margaree – her silent bit of revenge.

Cecilia wouldn't be like that, Jeannie thought. *We'd be best friends, but she'd be nice to everybody else, too. Like Mary in* The Secret Garden. *And she'd be fun, like Jo in* Little Women, *but she wouldn't be silly.*

Cecilia would be the perfect friend . . . if she were real. Jeannie had made her up from the best parts of all the best characters in books.

Once a month, Jeannie's father drove her to the one-room library at Inverness. She'd read every book the librarian would allow her. She'd read her favorites over and over.

Cecilia would love to read, of course. She'd like making clothes, too. Jeannie wished Cecilia were real so she could help with the hemming. Jeannie hated hemming. And, she had decided, they would be the very same height.

"I wish you were here," Jeannie said aloud. All she could do was wish.

She set the blueberry pails down on the dusty path to ease her fingers and plucked a last late dandelion puff. She whispered, then blew on the seed head. Her wish drifted out over the hillside, became part of the haze, and disappeared.

She picked up the pails and headed home.

2

At the bottom of the hill, Jeannie took the stream path through the woods. The darkness was a relief, but the air was still heat-scorched, heavy with the smell of baking spruce needles, and with the high whine of insects. To either side of the path, a fierce tangle of sharp branches and deadwood barred entry. Shadows moved and branches sighed against each other, but Jeannie took no notice. Every shape and smell and sound of the forest was familiar to her.

She ducked around a last cloud of mosquitoes and came out into her own yard. Barn and sheds, house and yard, all stood together in a cosy half circle. Across the road, their farm fields and meadows began again, hard-fought for and won again each year against the return of the old forest that stretched in every direction.

The Shaw home was comfortable, cheerful, and growing. Mama was having another baby, and Daddy was adding two rooms to the house. He had paying work for the summer – one of the few steady jobs for a lot of local men since the war ended seven years ago – clearing brush for power lines that would finally come through the valley. Her father was using the cash to buy nails and roofing.

"Hi, Daddy," Jeannie called, hearing him in the depths of their faded red barn.

"Hello, Jeannie," he called back. "Hot enough for you on the hill?"

"It was awful." She stepped into the hay-dusted darkness. "Where are you?"

"We're in the workshop. Come rescue me from my 'assistant' here!"

Jeannie's little sister popped her head out. "I'm helping Daddy make a new axe handle," Pearl announced. "She's a beaut! Daddy says so. Come see, Jeannie."

"That's nice, Pearl. I better get these berries inside before they cook right here. Anyway, I'm still not talking to you."

Pearl ignored her sister's last words. "You look cooked, too, Jeannie. You look like a steamed pudding!"

"Gee, thanks."

Jeannie carried the pails across the yard. She stopped

to scratch the head of their beagle, Lady. "Hello, old girl," she said. The dog opened her eyes, but didn't move.

Lady used to race through the summer, ears flapping, wildly excited by every grasshopper. As soon as Pearl had learned to walk, the dog followed her everywhere. Now Lady was old, and there was as much gray in her fur as there was black and tan. She lay in the same spot on the veranda most of the time, where the boards were a bit farther apart and cooler air could drift through.

Still, at some point each day, Lady would perk up her ears at the high lilt of Pearl's voice. She'd pick herself up and go find Pearl, wherever she had wandered off. Satisfied with a pat on her head, Lady would plod back to the veranda and sleep the afternoon away.

Mama opened the screen door for Jeannie. "Sit down before you fall down," she said. "I'll get you a drink." She cranked the pump handle at the enamel sink. Jeannie drank the cool springwater, then held the glass against her cheek.

Mama pushed a cast-iron pan of fried bologna to the back of the woodstove. She stirred a jam pot and returned to rolling pastry at the big table. Her apron curved over her belly as she leaned forward to work. The baby was due before Christmas.

"Your cheeks are as red as mine feel," Jeannie commented. "Why are you even baking?"

"Pies don't bake themselves," Mama replied. "Two of these are for the Church Supper. I might as well bake for us, too."

"I wish we could get one of those electric stoves," Jeannie said. "Couldn't we, Mama, when the power lines come through? Think how cool the kitchen would stay."

"'If wishes were horses, beggars would ride.' There won't be power in this house for a few years yet. Your father's pay won't stretch to that. Anyway, I can't imagine baking without my woodstove. Come on, now. 'Many hands make light work.'"

Jeannie splashed her face with tepid water from the holding pan in the sink. "I'll be right back," she said.

It was just as hot upstairs. She pulled off the limp ribbon and brushed until the waves tidied a little. "Awful hair," she told her reflection.

She unknotted a ribbon from the tangle she'd thrown on her bed that morning. It made her cross all over again. She'd discovered the ribbons after breakfast, linked in a chain across her mirror. Pearl's handiwork.

Pearl was learning to tie her shoes and she loved to practise: on aprons, Daddy's boots, Jeannie's ribbons. And they all ended in knots more often than bows.

It was the first time in her life Jeannie had pocket money for anything, let alone a luxury like new hair ribbons. Her clothes were almost all hand-me-downs from cousins. The dresses she'd made herself this summer were the first new clothes she'd had in years. It felt wonderful to put on a dress that no one else had ever worn! Campbell's Store had a perpetual sale on sewing goods. With twenty-five cents from selling a pail of blueberries, Jeannie could buy the two yards of material, ten cents a yard, buttons and thread extra.

The first time she'd had two cents to spare, she had hovered over the ribbons; had felt their perfect smoothness, shiny and so richly colored. She stood there so long, unable to choose, savoring the treat of being able to choose, and finally bought a length of creamy yellow. The next week, she'd bought royal blue. Now she had five ribbons lined up on her bureau, like samples from a rainbow.

And Pearl couldn't keep her hands off them.

Not that Jeannie hadn't warned her, and complained to their mother, too. But she got into more trouble for tattling and for yelling at her sister than Pearl got into for her mischief.

"That brat," Jeannie mumbled.

Her mother was testing the jam when Jeannie came downstairs and stood in the doorway, with the cool dark hall behind her and the wall of wet heat ahead.

"There you are," Mama said. "I thought you must've gone to sleep, you took so long. Mash these potatoes, please. Then wash those blueberries so I can get them cooked. This batch is nearly ready."

Jeannie tied an apron on and began to work. Steam rose from the bowl of potatoes, and from the pot of jam. "Oh, Mama, it's too hot in here."

"You're right," Mama said. "Let's go sit in the stream and cool off. These berries can wait until October. I expect they'll be fuzzy by then, all slippery and rotten, but –"

"Stop!" Jeannie begged. "Why do you have to say such silly things, Mama?"

" 'Good cheer is the best physician.' "

"Yesterday you told us, 'The best physician is apple pie and cheese.' "

"Yesterday," Mama said, "you weren't old enough to correct your mother." She wiped a hand and patted Jeannie's head. "Such lovely hair."

"It's not lovely. It's terrible! I wish I had straight hair like the rest of you. And I wish you'd get cross at Pearl! My ribbons were knotted into a chain this morning, you know."

"Yes, dear, you told me. Since when did you start fussing over your hair, anyway? And these ribbons! I'd have thought you'd treat yourself to candy once in a while, like any self-respecting child."

"Mama, I am twelve . . . almost."

"Yes, you are. How did that happen?"

The jam bubbled and Mama went to tend the pot. Jeannie tugged at the apron. "Feels like I'm wearing my winter coat," she muttered.

"All right, all right," Mama declared, rapping her wooden spoon on the pot rim. "I suppose you've done enough by picking."

Jeannie couldn't believe her luck and began peeling off the heavy apron.

"But," her mother went on, "as a trade, I need you to take my place this evening, serving the Church Supper."

No wonder Jeannie had been allowed to escape the kitchen work.

"Raising money for the new stove is a worthy cause," Mama said, "but I'm sure they won't mind if I don't waddle around, getting in the way. Daddy can take you there and pick you up after he gets the truck seen to at the garage."

Jeannie's heart sank. *It'll be nothing but church women and the reverend,* she thought. She would have pleaded not to go, but one look at her mother's tired face shut her up.

"Sure, Mama," she said.

"That's my girl. Go tell Daddy dinner's ready if he is."

When Jeannie returned from the barn, Mama was laying a top crust on the last pie. "Hope this pastry is decent," Mama said. "I wouldn't want the ladies of the parish saying, 'Poor Mrs. Shaw. Can't bake to save her life!'"

"Everyone knows you're a good cook."

"And everyone knows," Mama said, "you ought to make pastry on a cool day. But, 'needs must,' as they say."

"Daddy and the Pest will be right in," Jeannie told her. "Can I iron the knots out of my ribbons until it's time to sit down?"

"It's 'may I.' Yes, you may. I see you can stand the heat when it's your own ribbons."

"Well," Jeannie offered, "'needs must' . . . as they say." Her mother wagged a floury finger at her.

Jeannie lifted the heavy irons to the front of the stove. By the time she'd set up the ironing board across the tops of two chairs and brought the ribbons from her room, the flatirons were hot. She held up the chain of knotted ribbons for her mother to see.

Mama sighed. "I know, Jeannie. Very creative, you must admit. I can't keep up with that child lately."

Jeannie unknotted the first ribbons. She dipped her fingers in water and sprinkled one, then hooked an iron with the wooden handle.

She and Mama jumped when the screen door was flung open and slammed shut. "I'm here!" Pearl shouted.

"Pearl!" Mama exclaimed as she put the pie down. "You'll be the death of me, or at least of this pie. Go wash your hands. Oh, dear. It didn't take you long to dirty your dress."

"That's clean dirt, Mama," Pearl informed her. "Worker dirt."

Mama shook her head. Jeannie thumped a heavy iron onto another ribbon. *No matter what Pearl does,* she fumed to herself, *Mama forgives her.*

When that iron cooled, Jeannie returned it to the stove to reheat and lifted the next one. "Pearl," she began, "look what I have to do over again because of you. I just ironed these yesterday."

Pearl picked up the knotted ribbons. "But they were so pretty on your mirror."

Jeannie got ready to say a lot more, but Mama stopped her with "Dinner in peace, please." Jeannie pinched her lips together.

By the time Daddy sat down to remove his boots, Jeannie had draped her finished ribbons across the ironing board. She went to the well and leaned in to reach the crock where the butter dish and milk pitcher were kept. She hugged their coolness to her as she carried them.

"Pearl Shaw!" she cried as she came in.

Daddy was tipped back in his old chair by the door, drinking tea from his big mug . . . and decorated with Jeannie's ribbons. Two were draped over his hair, two more looped through his buttonholes.

"Look!" Pearl said. "I'm making Daddy into a Christmas tree for you."

"Get those off Daddy!" Jeannie shouted. "Oh! You still haven't even washed your hands!"

Daddy sheepishly pulled off a ribbon, but said, "She meant no harm, Jeannie."

Mama came hurrying from the pantry. "Oh, dear, Pearl," she sighed.

"Is that it?" Jeannie cried. "Is that all she gets?"

"Jeannie," Daddy's quiet voice warned, "don't talk to your mother like that."

Jeannie swallowed past the lump in her throat. "My ribbons," she forced out, "are *not* for decorating Daddy."

Pearl's eyes filled with tears. "I wasn't hurting them!"

"Pearl," Mama said, "Jeannie's hands are full. Be a good girl and put her ribbons out of the way for her – but wash your hands first. And she's right, they're not for putting on Daddy. When we finish eating, you can be a big girl and learn to wash and iron them."

"Can I really? I'll make them all nice for you, Jeannie!" Pearl ran to the sink.

Mama turned to Jeannie. "'A soft answer turneth away wrath,'" she quoted.

Jeannie couldn't speak, since no soft answer came to her mind. She barely spoke during the meal, either.

As she dried the dishes, she thought instead of her blueberry money. With the quarter, she could buy material for a dress and another new ribbon for her hair.

How much more fun it would be, Jeannie thought, as she tipped dishwater onto the flower bed, *if I had someone to go with me to Campbell's Store. Cecilia would help choose material. Cecilia would understand what it's like to have a spoilt little sister, too!*

Jeannie walked, alone, up the long dirt road to Campbell's Store. In her mind, she sorted through the familiar bolts of cotton prints. *Which one should I choose?* she wondered. This would be one of the last times she'd have money in her pocket, until next blueberry season.

The bell jangled as she entered. "There you are!" Mrs. Campbell called from the stepladder. "I was hoping you'd bring me more berries today. Verity insists she doesn't have a spare moment for picking, not with school starting. But she does love my blueberry jam." She finished attacking the canned goods with her dust mop. "Don't know why I bother," she said as she climbed ponderously down. "By the time I finish these shelves, they're coated again. This is the driest, dirtiest summer since I was knee high to a dandelion."

Jeannie hoisted her pail onto the high wooden counter and lifted aside the dish towel.

"They're lovely, dear, as always," Mrs. Campbell pronounced. She whisked her metal cash box from under the counter. "Here you go – a shiny new 1952 quarter. Now what will you do with all that money?" she teased. "Spend it on candy?"

Jeannie hadn't even tasted candy since last Easter, when Nanny and Papa Shaw had sent Pearl and her each a little chocolate egg. Pearl had unwrapped hers and popped it right in her mouth. Jeannie had taken tiny bites, savoring every one. When the last taste of chocolate melted in her mouth, she had smoothed the creases out of the gold foil and tucked it under the glass of her bureau top, where it caught the sun each morning.

A quarter would have bought nearly a pound of penny candies.

Jeannie slipped the coin into her pocket and headed for the fabric counter.

"Going to sew another dress, are you, dear?" Mrs. Campbell said. "That last one you made, with the yellow daisies on it, would've cost you as much as $1.25, store boughten in Inverness!"

Mrs. Campbell poked her head around the curtain leading to their upstairs living quarters. "Verity," she called, "Jeannie Shaw is here. Come say hello and help her pick out material." She beamed at Jeannie. "You two can have a nice visit while I get back to this dusting."

Jeannie was relieved when there was no response from upstairs. Verity Campbell made her nervous.

She sorted through the bolts of fabric, unable to choose between the pale green with colored dots and the baby blue with flowers.

Mrs. Campbell shuffled back to the stairs and yelled, "Verity, get down here, I told you! Jeannie Shaw is here." She turned and smiled at Jeannie again. "All ready for Grade Seven, are you? You picked out some real nice items for school, all top of the line."

Jeannie was pleased, thinking of the school supplies she'd saved for and bought over the blueberry season. For once, she'd be as good as anyone starting back to school tomorrow.

A thunder of feet on the stairs and the Three-Headed Monster tumbled into the store, giggling as usual. Verity untangled herself from her two friends and eyed Jeannie. "Oh," she said, "it's you, Jeannie. Picking material?"

"That's okay, Verity," Jeannie said, "I'm just looking. Hi, Melanie. Hi, Sarah."

Sarah mumbled hello. Melanie merely looked at her.

Go away, go away, Jeannie kept repeating in her head.

"That one's not so bad," Verity said, when Jeannie returned to the pale green cotton with tiny, colored polka dots. "It'd be all right for bathroom curtains."

Jeannie frowned, but let the green material slide from her fingers.

19

Melanie giggled behind her hand. "Well, nothing going on here," she said. "We'll be upstairs. C'mon, Sarah. Don't be long, Verity."

When they were gone, Verity flopped onto the press-back chair behind the counter and fussed with wiping dust from her patent leather shoes. She had, Jeannie knew, at least four pairs of shoes. And Verity Campbell's socks *always* looked new and perfectly white.

Jeannie chafed at the way her pleasure in choosing material was being spoiled.

"What about this one?" It was Verity, leaning forward and pulling out the white with yellow daisies.

"I just made a dress with it," Jeannie said, and got ready for another insult.

"*Hmm*," said Verity. "I suppose that'd be pretty."

Jeannie opened her eyes wide. *Verity Campbell just gave me a compliment . . . sort of.*

"Well, how about this one?" Verity offered the soft blue with the tiniest blue and pink forget-me-nots sprinkled over. "It's the second nicest."

"I've been thinking of that one," Jeannie admitted. "Yes, okay. That's what I'll get. Thanks, Verity."

Jeannie followed her to the open counter, where Verity cut two yards from the bolt of cloth. The display box of ribbons lay open on the countertop. She touched the richness of the wide velvet ribbons at the back. "They're so pretty," she whispered.

"Yeah. Our best ribbon," Verity said. "We're getting it in a nice blue next time the salesman comes by. That's the color for me. So, do you want it or not?"

Wouldn't it be nice, Jeannie thought, *to choose anything I want the way Verity can?* But at five cents a yard, she couldn't afford fancy velvet ribbons. "No," she said aloud, "this'll be fine." Not exactly the right blue to match her new material, but it would have to do. Buying the material and the store's cheapest ribbon would take all her money.

"So," Verity continued, "are you all ready for school tomorrow?"

"I guess," Jeannie said. "I'm getting new shoes, but they haven't arrived yet. And I bought a new schoolbag. That one, see?" She pointed to the green canvas schoolbags hanging from a nail against the wall.

"Nice," Verity admitted. "I like the big pocket on the front and –"

"Are you coming or not, slowpoke?" Melanie demanded, appearing around the curtain again.

"Oh, be quiet," Verity snapped. "I'll be there in a minute."

But Melanie waited.

"Anyway," Verity told Jeannie, "I got *my* school supplies when we were in Halifax last month. Clothes, too. Must have spent nearly fifty dollars! They have so many stores and so much to choose from. Not like this boring old stuff." And she was gone, arms linked with Melanie's.

Jeannie glared after them, her cheeks burning. *Stupid girls!* she thought. She grabbed her piece of material and ribbon, hurrying to get out of there.

But the bell jangled again. Reverend Hope and his wife arrived, needing supplies for the Church Supper, and Mrs. Campbell always waited on her adult customers first. While she got a pound of sugar and a foil packet of Red Rose tea, Rev. Hope told them about the berry-picking excursion he was planning.

"I do hope," he told Jeannie, "you can join us. We all thank the good Lord, of course, that our returned soldiers are finally seeing some employment, but the season's almost over and a number of families haven't had transport out to the Barrens to pick yet. We'll rally the older boys to drive the wagons, and it should be a most pleasant event. I do hope the weather cooperates."

Jeannie grinned. Her father always called the minister Reverend I-Do-Hope. And riding to the Crowdis Barrens in horse and wagon, with a community picnic after, would certainly be fun. Her good mood returned.

Jeannie couldn't wait to tell Mama about the plans. She

hoped her mother would be willing to go. "Oh, Mrs. Hope," she remembered, "Mama can't come to the Supper tonight. But she's sending pies, and I'm coming to help instead."

"Your poor mother," Mrs. Hope exclaimed. "She must truly be suffering in this heat."

"You will certainly be as welcome as your mother's delicious pies," Rev. Hope said. "I wish there were more girls and boys with your spirit."

Jeannie was not looking forward to the evening. As if he'd read her thoughts, Rev. Hope added, "Still, I do hope I might find another youth to join you, among us old fogies."

Who will he find? It'd be awful if it were Melanie Matthews. And I don't want to see Verity again. Maybe Sarah Phillips; she's not so bad. Or cousin Tina. She can't seem to talk about anything but her wedding, but at least she's cheerful. I wish it would be Tina.

"We'd better get going, dear," Rev. Hope said to his wife. "I promised I'd go see Mrs. Parker. Her son's widow is visiting her, I do believe. If only poor Alf Parker had made it through the war," he went on, "but the dear Lord knows best. We'll have to hurry to get out there and back in time for the Supper. Don't worry, Jeannie, I'll do my best to find a friend to join you this evening."

Jeannie smiled politely. *Not much chance of that,* she thought.

As she was leaving with her parcel of ribbon and material, a panel truck parked in front of the store. Mrs. Campbell came out to see who the driver was, and to get a better look at the bureau and table tied to the truck roof.

The stranger climbed out and stretched. "Hello, ma'am," he said. "Can ya tell me the way to Mrs. Alf Parker's place?"

Mrs. Campbell peered past his shoulder into the dark depths of the truck. "There's a Mrs. Dan P. She'd be the only Parker around here now. Her son was Alf."

"That sounds about right," he said.

"It's some hot, isn't it? Come in and have an orange pop," Mrs. Campbell offered. "Where'd you say you come from?"

"Mama," Jeannie called as she came in the house, "there's going to be an outing to the Crowdis Barrens next Saturday. A picnic, too! Can we go? Rev. and Mrs. Hope say hello. A furniture man was looking for old Mrs. Parker's house. Look, here's the material I bought."

"What a lot of news," Mama said. "This cotton is lovely, dear. Put it by the sewing machine for now and go get ready for the Supper."

Jeannie carried the enamel pan of water outdoors. Lady sniffed at it before draping her head over the edge of the step again. Jeannie washed her face and neck, then peeled off her thin white sneakers and socks, grubby now with dust. With the pan on the lower step, she sat down and slipped her feet into the water.

She rested her chin on her folded arms and wiggled her toes, while she conjured her perfect, pretend friend, Cecilia. Like playing with paper dolls, she could switch hair color, choose outfits from the Eaton's catalogue. Sometimes Cecilia was a quiet girl, sometimes a chatterbox.

"Doesn't matter to me," Jeannie whispered to Lady as she patted the dog. "I'd like her no matter what."

Their noisy old truck announced its return long before it came into sight. Daddy tapped Jeannie on the head with his work gloves as he came up the steps. He smelled of hard work, hot sun, and forest.

"Met up with the reverend on the road," he said. "Says you'll be pleased to hear he's found someone your age to join you at the Church Supper."

"Who, Daddy?" Jeannie asked, flicking water with her toes. "It can't be Tina if she's my age."

"He wouldn't say. Said it was a surprise for you. Someone new, as a matter of fact."

Jeannie's foot shot out and the pan of water spilled onto the dry ground. Lady snuffled at the commotion and went back to sleep. "Someone new! How could there be someone new?" Jeannie demanded, rescuing the pan. "Who is it?"

Daddy held up his hands. "How should I know? He just said he-do-hope you two would become fast friends since you're the same age." He started to open the screen door. "Probably one of Alf Parker's kids. Phillips, at the garage, says Alf's widow brought her family back to live with his mother. I know they had a bunch of boys while they still lived here before the war. Suppose they're mostly grown, now. Phillips said something about girls, too, but seemed like he didn't know for sure. Must be her."

He went in. Jeannie could hear him, through the pantry window, repeating the news about the Parker family to her mother. She stared at the spot where Daddy had been standing when he told her.

She raced in on wet feet, flung the pan under the sink, and flew upstairs. She looked in her mirror, hands pressed to her mouth. "This is it!" she said. "She's here. And I'm going to meet her!"

She changed into her best dress – the white one with the daisies. She brushed her hair hard and tied it in a yellow ribbon.

When she came downstairs, Mama was ladling soup into bowls. "I can't eat supper," Jeannie said right away. "My stomach's gone all funny."

"Are you coming down with something?"

"No, Mama. I'm just excited about this new girl."

"Don't suppose you'll starve, then. They'll give you a

plate of food by the end of the evening, likely. We haven't seen Alf's family for years," Mama said as she sat down. "He was buried overseas, so there wasn't even a funeral. Last we heard was when we went out to pay our respects to his mother, poor soul."

Daddy buttered a hot biscuit. "Smartest boy in our class, even got a scholarship to Dalhousie, but Alf wouldn't leave Cape Breton. Took that job at Ben's Bakery in Sydney, when their fourth boy was born. He used to play his fiddle at the dances, remember, Priscilla? Never expected to see him in Halifax when I went to sign on with the North Novies. Poor Alf." Daddy shook his head. "The last spring of the war, on March 24, we were advancing along the Rhein, right inside Germany. Even Churchill was there watching. We lost more men that day. . . ."

Mama poured tea after supper. "What's made his wife come back here? I didn't think she and Alf's mother were all that close. Wasn't she staying with her people in Yarmouth? A sister, I think."

"Rev. Hope just said old Mrs. Parker wrote and asked her."

"Jeannie," Mama said, "Daddy tells me you'll be meeting one of them at the Supper. Don't be rude and ask a lot of questions. Just tell her we look forward to seeing them all. Funny, I didn't realize they had any girls. You be friendly, now."

Jeannie laughed at the idea. She didn't need to be told. The Parker girl and she were going to be best friends.

"Stay, Lady," Daddy commanded to the sleeping dog as he stepped around her on his way to the truck. Lady hadn't needed to be told that for two years now.

"That joke is as tired as that dog," Mama said. She laid the pies on the truck seat. "Be sure to apologize if the crusts are tough," she told Jeannie, "or if they sink."

"Would you stop?" Jeannie insisted. "The pies'll be fine. Let's get going, Daddy, before Mama won't let me take them at all."

He shifted into gear and called to his wife, "Don't worry, Priscilla. They can always use your pies as doorstops." He drove away. In the wildly vibrating side mirror, Jeannie could see her mother shaking her finger at the truck.

Daddy dropped Jeannie at the church hall. Sounds of dishes and voices drifted out as she climbed the steps. There seemed to be an awful lot of laughing.

I wonder if she's arrived yet, Jeannie thought. She paused at the top, when she caught sight of the first star. "Star light, star bright, I don't need to wish on you tonight."

Another burst of laughter had Jeannie smiling as she entered the hall. She looked up . . . and nearly dropped a pie.

Rev. Hope hurried over. "I told you I'd find another youngster to liven things up! Surprise!"

It *was* someone young, someone her own age. And it *was* a surprise – not Sarah, not Tina. And certainly not Cecilia.

It was a boy.

And the ladies were laughing as he entertained them by tying a frilly apron on himself.

"Jeannie Shaw," announced Rev. Hope, "this is Cap Parker. His family has just returned to live in the valley. I do hope you two will become good friends."

3

*F*riends? *With a boy . . . a boy who's making a fool of himself?*

"Hi," the boy said, the apron dangling from his neck.

Jeannie took a breath. She pasted a smile on her face. "Hello."

"I must admit," Rev. Hope was saying, "I was as surprised as you. Cap volunteered right away. Of course, it will give him a chance to meet some of the young fellows, but he was the answer to your prayers, wasn't he, Jeannie?"

Jeannie's face burned at the minister's choice of words. When she saw Cap grin, she spun away, almost flipping one of the pies onto him. He laughed, actually laughed.

How dare he? Her disappointment was bitter in her throat and her mind shut against him.

Cap took no notice. He went back to tying the apron.

He turned in circles, looking over his own shoulder like a puppy chasing his tail.

Look at them all, just about cooing over him. I'm embarrassed for him, she decided. She stomped away in disgust and delivered the pies to the kitchen, plunking them down hard on the table. *Mama doesn't have to worry – if they don't sink from that, they won't sink at all.*

And just as quickly she felt ashamed of herself.

What's wrong with me? It's not his fault he's a boy. Yes, but – stop it, stop it, stop it! Why do I always have to think so much? I bet no one else argues with themselves!

Mrs. Hope fluttered into the kitchen. "It's so nice, dear, to have you join us. I harbor a hope that you and Cap might encourage our youngsters to return to community service in these brighter days. Breathe new life into us!"

She would have continued in her poetic flow, but caught sight of Cap laying cutlery. "Cap, dear," she called, "forks to the left, knives to the right. Tell you what, why don't you start putting the chairs and benches out? That's boys' work. I'll show you where they're stored." And she fluttered out again.

Wonderful aromas came from all corners of the kitchen: turkeys being carved, vegetables being boiled, smoked hams arriving hot out of the ovens of Margaree Valley homes. The ladies chatted over the clatter of pots and pans.

"A very nice boy," Mrs. MacFarlane said. "Poor dear. I heard his family arrived with nothing but the clothes on their backs."

"That's not one bit true!" Mrs. Campbell informed her. "They may not have had more than a few suitcases when they got off the train at Orangedale. I wouldn't know about that; I mind my own business. But the rest of their belongings arrived this very day. I saw the truck myself. And with some nice things, too, from what I could see. The driver stopped to ask directions. I said, 'Son, that's easy. There's only one road from here, and you're standing on it. Drive 'til you run out of road. That'll be old Mrs. Parker's house at the end.'"

"But it's true they arrived under cover of night," insisted John Angus's mother. "I heard they landed on poor Alf's poor mother's doorstep, without so much as a –"

"Shame on you!" Mrs. Campbell lectured, shaking a gravy ladle. "Old Mrs. Parker sent for them. That's what Rev. Hope said, but don't mention I told you. And they arrived at night because that's when Dan P. Jr. could get them here. That'd be the oldest son, the one that came back from the war with the bad arm. He delivers for Ben's Bakery out of Sydney now, same as Alf did, God rest his soul. Dan P. had to make two trips because there were six or seven of them."

Jeannie got ready to ask whether there'd been a girl her

age among these six or seven, but Mrs. Campbell talked on as she whipped the gravy into shape. "Old Mrs. Parker wrote and offered to make a home for them. Company for her, I'd call it. They've been getting settled, out at the Parker place, Cap says. That's why they didn't come tonight. Not that I don't wonder how she's feeding so many without shopping at our store. She keeps herself to herself, which I always admire. Even Rev. Hope didn't know they were here to stay until he visited them this afternoon. The doctor was out there, too. You can't be too careful, you know."

Everyone stopped talking and kept working. Jeannie knew what their silence was about – polio. There hadn't been a single case in Inverness County – not yet, anyway – but everyone was too scared even to mention the terrible virus. *It's like an evil spirit reaching out,* Jeannie thought, as she saw the women's pinched lips. *If we keep quiet about it, maybe it won't find us here.*

She stepped forward, ready to use the silence to ask just how many Parker kids would be showing up for first day of school tomorrow. *And isn't it true at least one of them's a girl?*

"Now," Mrs. Campbell finished with a flourish of her ladle, "no more of your gossip. Work to do, ladies!" She hoisted a huge pot off the stove and over to the sink to drain.

Jeannie didn't dare question her now. "What should I be doing?" she asked the aproned backs instead. It was all so busy and everything in such large quantities. Mrs. Campbell tipped out an avalanche of steaming potatoes into a bowl the size of a washtub.

"There you are, dear." Mrs. Campbell thrust a potato masher into Jeannie's hands. "Make sure to get out all the lumps. Our diners do not approve of lumps."

Jeannie hefted the utensil. "It's as big as a shovel!" she said. She found an apron, washed her hands, and started mashing.

She was relieved when Mrs. Phillips eyed her efforts and said, "Lovely, dear. Let me just finish them off for you. Why don't you put out the salt and pepper shakers?"

That was something she could handle. She carried the basket around and put two sets of shakers on each long table. The noise of chairs and tables being dragged into position filled the hall.

"Hi, Jeannie," Cap called from the other side of the echoing room.

"Hello," Jeannie answered, not even looking up from her work. She struggled with the thought that she'd have to speak directly to this boy if she wanted to find out about his sister.

Cap set chairs in line at a far table. "I wondered where you'd hidden yourself," he called.

Jeannie's head snapped up. "I certainly was not hiding!"

"Fine," he said. "Things sure smell great in the kitchen, don't they?"

She tried to swallow the flash of irritation before she went over to talk to him.

"Hope there's enough left for us," he offered over the noise.

Jeannie still said nothing. *There, that's the last salt and pepper shakers to set out.* Now she would make herself speak to him. She started across the floor.

Cap slammed a last bench into position and started across the hall, too. "Look here, Jeannie Shaw," he began, "I don't know why you're so darn snooty, but –"

And at that very same moment, the first people stepped into the hall, between Jeannie and Cap, for the Wilson United Church Turkey and Ham Supper Fund-raiser for the new stove. Mrs. Campbell swooped out of the kitchen to greet them.

Cap Parker glared at Jeannie. Jeannie glared back. But he was sent to assist Mrs. Hope in collecting admissions at the door – twenty-five cents for adults, ten cents for children – and to be introduced to all as "poor Alf's son." Everyone in the hall was talking about his family returning to the valley. Jeannie refused to listen to another word about him. Snooty, he'd called her. She'd never been so insulted.

They were both kept busy. Jeannie lined up to collect plates of dinner to serve. Cap was scooping mashed potatoes.

"That's way too much!" Jeannie told him.

"Says who?" he challenged.

Mrs. Hope looked over and said, "Just make sure that plate goes to a man, Jeannie. Cap, dear, a tad less generous so we can serve everyone."

Ooh, Jeannie fumed, *just like my mother with Pearl, always letting her off the hook.*

When Jeannie began clearing dirty plates, Cap came out to do the same.

"You're going to break those!" Jeannie warned. Where she and the ladies stacked three high at most, Cap piled six plates and more, cutlery and all. At first, onlookers gasped to see him, but watching him balance, stagger, almost lose the stack, then recover – that became the entertainment. Each safe journey was marked by an ever more energetic cheer, especially from the boys who'd hung around, way longer than they normally would, to meet the new boy.

The more the diners cheered, the more Rev. Hope beamed, and the more Jeannie fumed. *He just gets here and settles right in. How does he do that?*

At the end of the evening, Rev. Hope said, "Jeannie,

my dear, I want to thank you for all your work. Your mother can be proud." Jeannie could imagine what her mother would have to say about her daughter's lack of welcome for Cap.

"And," Rev. Hope continued, "my wife informs me we almost ran out of food, attendance was so high! Word has spread that Alf's family is back. Thought they might be here this evening, it seems. But at least Cap is. And so likeable. He has made this the most successful Church Supper we've ever had!"

Jeannie's smile disappeared. *Cap Parker, Cap Parker. That's all anyone can talk about! What has he done that's so wonderful, anyway?* She yanked off the apron and thrust it at the bewildered minister. "Here," she said. "I have to go."

She hurried to the door as Cap was crossing the floor with a stack of chairs. He glared at her again and she glared back.

Out in the dusk, Jeannie let out her breath at last. She hoped her father would get there quickly. A car drove up, but it was Father MacNeil from the Catholic church. He had his fiddle and bow tucked under his arm.

"Hello, Jeannie," he said as he bounded up the steps. "I've come for a bit of ecumenical fiddle music with Rev. Hope to round off the evening. I wonder if Alf Parker's son is as musical as he was."

37

Jeannie was ready to scream. "I wouldn't know, Father," she said instead. "Anyway, I can't stay. I'm just waiting for my dad."

"That's a shame," he said as he entered the hall. "Bye, now, dear."

"So," Daddy asked on the ride home, "what's the Parker girl's name?"

"Wasn't a girl. A boy. Cap. What a stupid name." Jeannie avoided looking at her reflection in the truck window. She stared beyond to the black trees and sky.

"*Ah*," her father said. He rubbed his thumb across the dusty dashboard and checked the sky, too. "Sure could do with rain."

They rode in silence, but as soon as they got through the door, Mama made up for that. "Come here and tell me all about her."

"It wasn't a her," Jeannie said. "It was a him."

"That's too bad. Was the girl not able to come tonight? Oh, well, there's always tomorrow."

Jeannie's whole body perked up. *Of course there's a girl! She'll be a bit younger than Cap, that's all. I'll meet her at school tomorrow!*

Mama put her knitting down on her rounded tummy and said, "Come tell me all about the Supper. Pearl's finally in bed and I can hear myself think for a change."

Jeannie longed to go to bed herself and do some thinking about tomorrow, but she sat down on the needlepoint stool. She described the food, the crowd, the compliments of the diners. She repeated Mrs. Campbell's news about the Parker family. She even told how entertained everyone had been by Cap's silliness, leaving out only her argument with him.

Jeannie's eyelids began to droop. *Am I still speaking out loud, or are the words floating in my head?*

"You tell a grand story, Jeannie," Mama said. "As good as any on the radio. Now off to bed. School in the morning."

Jeannie fell asleep in the middle of making up a conversation between herself and the new girl, all about which was more annoying – older brothers or younger sisters.

4

S he was up just after dawn. It was too warm to lie in bed with her cotton nightgown clinging to her damp back. Her mother was feeding the chickens and her father had already left to cut brush.

Jeannie washed in cool water at the sink pump. Then upstairs again to get dressed.

Across the hall, Pearl sat up in bed and yawned. "School starts today," she said.

"I think I know that."

"Next year I'm going to school."

"I know that, too," Jeannie said. She pulled her white dress with the yellow daisies over her head, buttoned and smoothed it. *At least the Parker girl hasn't seen it yet.* A quick brush of her hair and the yellow ribbon.

"Anyway," Pearl challenged, "I get to play all day. And

Ella's coming over." Ella Ingraham was their other cousin, the same age as Pearl. "We're gonna play. All day."

"That's nice."

"How many wake-ups 'til I can start school?"

"Don't know."

Pearl padded down the stairs behind her.

"Breakfast is on the stove," Mama called, on her way to the garden.

Jeannie sighed. *Who can eat porridge in this heat, especially since Daddy made it more than an hour ago?* But that was breakfast from the morning school started, through winter, and straight on to grading day, no matter what. She plopped thick porridge into a bowl and smothered it in brown sugar and milk.

After she ate, she sharpened her new pencils with the paring knife. She checked again that the new scribblers, the new ruler, eraser, and scissors were ready in her brand-new schoolbag. All new. Jeannie could barely stop touching them.

Neither could Pearl.

"Leave my things alone," Jeannie ordered over her shoulder as she washed the breakfast dishes. "Put that down!" she demanded as she swept the kitchen floor.

"I didn't do anything," Pearl insisted. "I was just practising." With Jeannie standing in front of her, hands on hips, Pearl reluctantly slipped the strap of the schoolbag off over her head.

"When I start school," Pearl declared, "I'm going to have one just like this."

Once she'd rescued her schoolbag, Jeannie went out to sit on the step with Lady.

Finally it was time. "Bye, Lady. Bye, Mama!" She kissed her mother and ran down the drive.

She slowed as soon as she was out of sight. She didn't want to get to school before the new girl. That wasn't how she pictured it.

She won't know anyone. I'll walk right up to her and say hello. Soon as we see each other, we'll be friends.

When the older girls came into view ahead of her, Jeannie slowed even more. Sarah Phillips and Melanie Matthews leaned in, one on each side of Verity Campbell.

Jeannie tried not to worry about the girls getting to school ahead of her. *The new girl will be my friend,* she told herself, *I just know it. She'll be younger than Cap, that's all. Maybe already eleven, or her birthday's coming soon, like mine. We can go to each other's house for our birthdays! Daddy'll drive us. Maybe we'll give each other a present.*

As soon as the school yard came in sight, she started searching. The younger ones chased each other. The boys shoved each other. And the three girls were still talking, as if they hadn't been together every single day of summer. Not once did they speak to anyone else.

No new girl.

They live farther away, Jeannie considered. *So maybe they'll be late and I'll have to wait until recess to talk to her, but I'll save the seat next to me for her.* She stood on the step of the schoolhouse to watch the road, just in case. The yard was noisy with boys and girls yelling out their summer energy.

Miss MacQueen, the Junior Room teacher, swept out of her classroom. Queen of the Babies, the students called her. She asked how Jeannie's family was, then took up her post at the school door. Children crowded around and offered up a few younger brothers and sisters, who were the shy new pupils today.

The seniors' teacher and school principal was Mr. Moss, called Mousie by the older students – but never in his hearing. He was a runt of a man, bald except for a tuft above each ear. He'd be striding out any minute now to shake the life out of the school bell. *What a shame for the Parker girl to be late on her very first day.*

Jeannie stood on tiptoe when a car drove into view, but she knew right away it wouldn't be them. Not many people had cars. And everybody – even Verity – walked to school, no matter how far away they lived. The Parker family would do the same, through winter snow or spring mud.

"Jeannie Shaw," Miss MacQueen called, "tell Mr. Moss it's time for the bell, please."

Jeannie hated to leave her lookout post. She hated even more having to pass the three older girls on their way back from checking their hair in the speckled mirror of the cloakroom.

She was surprised when Verity actually spoke to her. "Nice dress, Jeannie. It'd look pretty on a girl with blonde hair." Verity flipped her own smooth golden mane as she sauntered past. Jeannie felt like a squashed bug as the other girls pushed by to follow Verity.

She entered the darkness of the hall between the two classrooms. Mousie was talking with someone in Senior Room.

Of course, Jeannie thought, *the new girl! All this time I've been worrying she'd be late. She was probably here early to meet the teacher. That's something I'd do.*

But the voice that answered Mousie was a boy's.

Oh. Cap Parker, she thought crossly. *Well, I guess he and his sister would talk to the principal together. After all, he'll be in Grade Seven with me, whether I like it or not. Never mind him. Please let her be in at least Grade Six so she'll be in Senior Room with us!*

She heard chairs scrape. Jeannie backed into the cloakroom. She'd let them pass and then come out as if by chance.

"All right, young man," Mousie was saying. "I'll keep that quiet for now, too. I'm not happy about it, as I said, but if it makes life easier. . . ."

Jeannie frowned. *Keep what quiet?*

"Thanks, sir." That was Cap.

Man and boy came into view ahead of her, two silhouettes in the hall doorway. No one else. Jeannie backed farther in, but there was no room left. She sagged down onto the low boot bench.

When Mousie rang the bell, students lined up and filed into the two classrooms. Jeannie fiddled with her schoolbag until they shuffled past. Then she put her chin up and entered the Senior Room last.

Mousie was pulling the big white register from the top drawer of his desk. He glanced at Jeannie as she stood at the back of the room, then nodded for her to take the remaining empty seat . . . right beside Cap Parker at a double desk.

As she took her place, wishing she were invisible, Jeannie saw Cap frowning at her. Then she stared straight ahead.

Mousie began to call the register, loudly and ceremoniously, as he always did on first day.

"Verity Campbell?"

"Present." *First as always,* Jeannie noted, *first in everything.*

"John MacDonald?"

"Here, sir," John Angus answered.

"Dougald MacFarlane?"

"Here."

"Melanie Matthews?"

"Here."

There was a pause. It had to be Cap next. "*Umm,* Chris. . . ." Mousie hesitated, as if he couldn't read his own writing for once. "Chris . . . topher Parker?" He peered over the huge register.

The class looked around at the new boy, then swiveled back to sit at attention.

"Christopher Parker," Mr. Moss said again. Even Jeannie looked over.

Cap nodded at the principal. "Yes, sir. Here."

"Yes," Mousie agreed back, and went on to finish with Sarah Phillips and Jeannie Shaw.

"First," their teacher announced, "I'd like to welcome Cap to our school. We are certainly glad to have the Parker family back among us. Your brothers did well here, and your father was one of this school's finest students, Cap. We were deeply saddened by his passing, but will be proud of him always." Mr. Moss removed his glasses, then put them right back on. "Now," he continued, "with the coming at long last of electrical power to the valley, we shall take up the study of electricity this term." He pointed to a list of vocabulary words already on the chalkboard.

Jeannie shuffled in her seat, trying to gather her courage. The last thing she wanted to do was speak to Cap Parker ever again, but she had to know. When Mousie turned to the board, she hissed to Cap, "Where's your sister?"

Cap stared at her. "What? I don't have a sister."

No sister. There it is, then. Daddy was wrong, and I was wrong, so wrong. The gray empty school year stretched out ahead of her.

Cap still leaned toward her, whispering something else. "Cousins," he said.

"What?"

"My cousin, I mean. Her dad died this spring. My aunt's working at the chocolate factory in Halifax, so Moira's staying with us for now."

"Well, where is she?"

"At home," Cap mouthed. He checked that the teacher was still busy. "She'll start next year. She's only four. Hey! My grandmother says your sister's four, too."

Jeannie stared at him, then slumped in her seat. "Great!" she mumbled. "Pearl gets another friend? Just my luck."

"Look here, Jeannie Shaw –" Cap started to say.

"Oh, be quiet!" Jeannie said louder – right into a silence as their teacher finished explaining the Latin meaning of "electric." *Elektricus,* he'd written on the board, *produced from amber by friction.*

Without looking around, Mousie called, "Miss Shaw, I trust you can wait to make Mr. Parker's further acquaintance at a more suitable moment?"

The whole class snickered but quickly subsided when Mousie turned his frown on them.

Jeannie sat rigid in her seat, on fire with embarrassment.

Whatever Mr. Moss said about electricity after that was lost on her. The awful morning dragged on. Cap's mumbled "sorry" didn't help when she finally forced her stiff body from her seat at recess.

"Don't you dare feel sorry for me!" she snapped.

He lifted his hands in exasperation. "I give up! Girls!" he said in disgust. He strode off to join the boys.

Jeannie glared at the floor, at the school step, then at the ground as she walked away to sit alone on the grassy hillock, turning her back on the school. She did the same at lunch. No one came after her. She could barely swallow the tiny bites of her fried egg sandwich.

A hard knot twisted inside her. It would be with her for the whole school year, she was sure. And it was all Cap Parker's fault. She was pretty sure of that, too.

CHAPTER

5

*J*eannie avoided the new boy all week. The rest of
the class hung around Cap at lunch and as soon as
they were released from school. They demanded details
of town life – of soda shops and sidewalks, electricity
everywhere, and movie theaters.

Cap Parker entertained them, recounting the plots of
Saturday movies. In turn, he wanted to hear about fishing
in the Margaree Valley. He grilled them about where they
went hiking. The girls wandered away, already bored. Just
another boy talking about hunting and fishing.

"Hiking?" John Angus shook his head at Cap. "Hiking's
for Boy Scouts!" The rest of the boys joined in the laugh.

They don't fool me, Jeannie thought, as she entered the
school yard. *They'd be first in line, I bet, if a Boy Scout
troop started up.*

"We go fishing," John Angus insisted. "We set traps and snares. We're men, not Boy Scouts!"

"Okay, then," Cap said. "Where's the best fishing? What kind of traps do you use?"

They fell over each other telling him what they knew, arguing. Their cheerful, loud voices carried all around the school yard to where Jeannie sat alone, trying not to hear them, hearing every word.

Cap brought his father's compass the second day, tucked in his shirt pocket with its cord looped through a buttonhole and knotted to a button. "That's the way my dad wore it," he told the boys, "so he wouldn't lose it."

On the third morning, he brought his dad's ordnance survey map of Inverness County. He used it in his presentation on "What I Accomplished During My Vacation." Mousie assigned that topic every September.

First, Verity recounted each detail of her trip to Halifax: the parks, the stores, a movie she'd seen. They even ate in a Chinese restaurant, though Verity had only French fries. Next, John Angus told about working in his grandfather's sawmill. And Melanie talked about her visits to all her relatives. It sounded as if she'd taken a dozen trips, but Jeannie knew Melanie Matthews' aunts and uncles and grandparents all lived on the very same street in Port Hood, about two hours away.

"The main thing I accomplished," Cap told the class

when his turn came, "was finally moving back to the Margaree Valley. Now every day I climb a mountain, or follow a stream, or walk the trails my father walked, before he went to war and died."

He went to war and died. Jeannie's heart hurt when Cap said it. *It could have been my father who never came home,* she thought. *I'm sure I'd die myself if that happened.*

What had it felt like even to have Daddy away during the war years? She shook her head. She'd been too young. She could barely remember the day he'd returned, looking like a tired version of the photograph he'd mailed from Halifax before shipping out. It had taken her, at five years old, over a week to stop hiding behind Mama every time he came in the room.

Jeannie shivered. It didn't seem real to think of losing anyone she cared about. She was glad the war was over so she wouldn't ever have to face such a thing.

"I think of my dad when I'm out in these woods," Cap read from his essay. "I was only three when he left for the war. But he wrote piles of letters home while he was overseas – pages and pages about where he'd take us in this valley. He said it was the best place in the world.

"And I was five when he died. I get my brothers to talk about him, about hunting and fishing with him. I heard the stories and read the letters so many times, I feel like I was on those trips with him. But I was too young to go."

Cap held himself still and easy at the front of the room – not like the other students, who had shuffled and sniffed and looked like they were caught in a trap.

"Now we've moved back to the Margaree Valley," he read, "like Dad always wanted us to do. I'm finding the rivers and trails myself, but it feels like I've been to them before. Because of my dad." Cap stopped reading, but he kept his head down. He ended the essay with, "He left Cape Breton to serve his country, but his heart was always here."

Goose bumps rose on Jeannie's arms. Nobody had ever talked about their island, or their fathers, that way before.

Jeannie watched Cap out of the corner of her eye as he sat down. He'd seemed so confident while he was up there, yet now she could see the redness around his neck.

The teacher cleared his throat. "An excellent effort," he said. "A credit to your writing skill . . . and to your father." Mousie got out his handkerchief, took off his glasses, and worked hard at polishing them. He called for Sarah Phillips to come up and give her talk.

Jeannie would speak last, as always, in the alphabetical order of the class, and couldn't wait to get it over. *What have I done in the summer, after all, except make clothes, pick blueberries, and sit on my favorite rock, wishing for a friend?* There was no way she'd tell about the hours she'd sat there, alone.

When it was finally her turn, Jeannie rushed through it, wearing one of the dresses she'd made, to show them. By now, the class was afternoon-sleepy. They paid as much attention to her talk as to the flies buzzing on the windows.

After school, Cap held the map open and asked John Angus, "Is this the river bend you meant, where the salmon pool is?"

Jeannie heard him, ahead of her, as they filed out of the classroom. Cap had looked up all the sites the boys had told him about, plotting distances and elevations for each one.

"You guys grew up knowing this stuff," he said on Friday morning, when she wandered by at recess. "I gotta make up for just moving back."

There wasn't a detail of the Margaree Valley, Jeannie could tell, that didn't fascinate him: its hills and folds, its wildlife and weather. It sounded as if he barely went home except to sleep. He'd discovered their father's heavy old canoe in the barn and had pestered his brothers to help him repair it. Already he'd dragged his brother Tam on a trip down the southwest branch of the Margaree River.

"You crazy?" Dougald challenged. "You musta had to carry the darn canoe more than paddle it! The water's too low this summer."

A few extra portages weren't going to stop him, Cap insisted. He told the boys about seeing a female moose, still as a statue, chomping on marsh grasses where the river opened up, just above Margaree Harbor. "Tam and I drifted past her," he recounted, "silent as fish. She was a beaut! First time I saw one in the open like that."

Jeannie hovered around the edges of the group, at the farthest distance their voices would carry, looking more interested in her library book than in any stupid boys talking. She would have loved to hear more about canoeing . . . if it weren't for the fact that she wasn't speaking to Cap.

"Aw, that's nothin'," John Angus was bragging. "I seen more darn moose than you can shake a stick at. They're dumber than dodoes, too. She wouldn'ta moved if you'd come up and kicked her in the bum!"

"Moose aren't dumb!" Cap said. "That she-moose knew there was nothing to worry about. Even a black bear won't take on a full-grown moose, y'know! My dad told me. Well, he told my brothers. Anyway," he continued, "we saw lots of bald eagles, too. One grabbed a salmon right out of the water. Right beside us!"

Mr. Moss called to Cap from the school doorway. Jeannie watched Cap wave to the departing boys and run to the step.

Cap pulled some papers out of his geography book

and gave them to their teacher, who looked them over, then shook his head. Cap shrugged. *What are they talking about?* Jeannie wondered. Mr. Moss gave Cap a schoolbook. Jeannie could tell it was the geography textbook they'd been issued three days ago. Cap tucked it in with his own copy. He nodded at the teacher and left the step.

When Cap passed Jeannie, he immediately shifted the books to his farther side.

Now, why would you need two copies of the same book? she wondered.

Back home, after doing the supper dishes, Jeannie made her way through the woods to the stream, to her rock. Lady used to keep her company, upsetting the frogs with her nosy sniffing, then settling in the cool damp grass. Now, even when Jeannie coaxed her, Lady wouldn't budge from the shade of the veranda.

"She's too old," Daddy had said.

"She's the same age as me!" insisted Jeannie.

"You know that's old in dog years, honey. These days, she makes more noise asleep than awake. Her sniffer doesn't sniff so good anymore. She's old and tired. Let her rest." Lady hadn't even gone rabbit hunting with Daddy last season. So Jeannie headed to her rock alone.

It was taller than she was, wider at the top than at its waterworn base. Two creases in its lumpy side offered footholds, now that she'd grown tall enough. Jeannie had come each spring to test her reach until she'd finally managed, on tiptoe, to pull herself up. That day it had become her rock. Curves in the top formed two natural seats. Sometimes Jeannie pretended Cecilia was sitting beside her.

That evening she climbed up and settled in the shade, not yet opening her book. She thought about her first week of school, about the new boy. *If it weren't for Cap Parker,* she'd told herself all week, *I'd have had someone to bring here.* Now, in this quiet place, she admitted he wasn't as awful as she'd sworn he was, and it wasn't his fault she didn't have a friend. The stream murmured to her. She forgave Cap for taking the place of the friend she'd wished for, and felt better.

Jeannie flipped open her Nancy Drew book, *The Mystery of the Tolling Bell.* An hour passed, while she imagined being along on the adventure. She finished the last chapter and closed the book. *Nancy Drew was so lucky. She always had her girlfriends, Bess and "George," to help her solve the case and to chum around with.*

She hadn't known how much she envied such friendship, not until her older cousin Tina had gone on to high school. Now Tina had passed Grade Eleven, left school, and become engaged, all in the same week. School days had become a series of lonely walks for Jeannie.

Not that she and Tina had been very close. She'd never asked her to come here, to her rock in the stream. Her cousin had taught her to sew; they'd had that to talk about and not much more. Now, with Tina planning her wedding and working at the fish plant in Inverness, Jeannie almost never saw her. She hadn't really minded at first. Not until this week, when school started.

Maybe I should try to stay friends with Tina after all. It has to be better than having no friend. That's what I'll do, first chance I get.

Jeannie tucked her legs up and rested her chin on her knees. She watched the stream until the mosquitoes came out at dusk. Once the first star appeared, she headed home.

On the Saturday morning of the blueberry outing, there was a rush at the Shaw house to finish breakfast, pack a lunch, gather berry buckets and a picnic blanket. The whole family crowded into the truck and Daddy dropped them off at the church hall before he headed out to clear brush.

The day was already hot as families gathered and caught up on news. When the steady *clip-clop* of hooves told them the wagons were arriving, a cheer went up. John Angus waved from the high seat of one wagon, then turned his attention to guiding the huge horse. Cap Parker drove the other.

Wouldn't you know, thought Jeannie. She crossed her arms and frowned. Pearl tugged at her sister. "Who's that?" she asked. "Is that poor Alf's boy, the one whose daddy died?"

Jeannie grabbed her sister's hand, found their mother, and herded them toward John Angus's wagon. Tina and Ella were already in that one with their mother, anyway. Auntie Libby patted the space next to her for Mama. Pearl and Ella sat on the board floor. Jeannie and Tina shared a space on the bench nearby.

When the boys called to their horses, they started off to another cheer. There was lots of lively chatter, especially in the other wagon, as they lumbered along the road. Jeannie stood, holding on to the rough wood, and poked her head up to see what was causing such excitement ahead of them. People were laughing at Cap's attempts to speed the horse, which ignored him as it plodded on. Cap was half turned on the wagon seat, laughing along with his passengers.

Jeannie's wagon jolted over a pothole and she flung her arms out for balance. The movement caught Cap's attention. He was looking right at her. Jeannie ducked down so quickly she sat on Pearl, who shoved her off.

Pearl stood and said, "What did you see, Jeannie? Oh. Hi, Cap Parker!" she yelled. Jeannie yanked on her sister's arm and toppled her. Pearl complained. Mama told them both to hush and be nice. The heat and rocking motion soon lulled everyone.

At last the Crowdis Barrens spread out around them – a wide, wild place. Rev. Hope and Mrs. Campbell called out to each other, one in each wagon, politely arguing over where the traditional stopping point was, until Cap settled it by stopping halfway between. Children jumped off. Older folks stretched and helped each other down.

Jeannie and Tina walked along a path until they were well out on the Barrens.

"So, how are the wedding plans going?" Jeannie began, although she already knew from her mother's and aunt's constant talks.

"Oh, Jeannie!" Tina exclaimed. "It'll be the second Saturday in June. Just think, in exactly forty weeks, I'll be Mrs. Edwin MacDonald . . . a married woman! Isn't that perfect?"

Jeannie could barely imagine being a high school student, let alone married, but she smiled and nodded as Tina planned her wedding suit, her flowers, her reception. She was walking on the Barrens, but flipping through the Eaton's catalogue in her mind as she listed what she would order for her perfect married life. She knew the page number of every item.

Jeannie tried changing subjects. "These berries are so yummy. Blueberry pie is my favorite dessert. What's yours, Tina?"

Tina clapped her hands. "That reminds me of the most perfect thing! Edwin's mother has set me to copying out all her recipes. I'll be able to serve my husband his favorite meals when he gets home from work. Isn't that heavenly?" Tina went all dreamy again. She moved from one bush to another, unaware of what she was picking.

"*Hmph,*" Jeannie muttered. "She'll be baking her husband twig pie, by the looks of it."

Tina kept chattering. And chattering.

"Tina," Jeannie said. "TINA! Oh, for heaven's sake," she exclaimed as her cousin kept babbling about Edwin, Edwin, Edwin!

Jeannie frowned at her. *Does falling in love make you this silly?* she asked herself. *I give up.* "Tina," she called, "I'm going to see how Mama's doing."

Tina looked around at last. "How is Aunt Priscilla, anyway? Imagine, Jeannie, in a few years, I'll be a mommy to my own dear little baby. Won't that be perfect?"

Jeannie left Tina listing Edwin's handsome features and the perfect children they'd have together.

"There you are," Mama said. "Isn't this a perfect day?"

"Please, Mama," Jeannie begged. "That's the only word Tina knows, besides Edwin."

"Ah, young love," Mama said as she stood up, and nearly fainted. "Oh, my. This heat is atrocious!"

"Sit down, Mama, on that rock. You should've stayed home and rested."

"If I'd stayed home, I wouldn't have been resting. That's one thing our Tina won't find perfect about looking after a home. 'Man may work from sun to sun, but woman's work is never done.' Still, it's a lovely day. Perhaps I'll sit awhile and enjoy it. I'll be fine."

Jeannie filled another pail before there was a common stirring and, next thing, everyone was unpacking lunches. Auntie Libby, Tina, and Ella spread their blanket nearby. They ate deviled ham sandwiches, cheese biscuits, and cookies.

"How come food tastes so good at a picnic?" Pearl asked, while nibbling the edges of a molasses cookie – her favorite kind. Mama lifted out the pickle jar of lemonade and poured it – warm from the sun, but tangy. "Look, Mama," Pearl said, "I'm drinking sunshine."

Jeannie said, "You've got sunshine dribbling down your chin, then." Pearl laughed.

Jeannie hated to admit it, but "perfect" was the word for this day. Everyone was happy with picnics and sunshine. Squirrels chittered from the bushes. A bald eagle called to its mate as they chased each other across the sky.

Rev. and Mrs. Hope came to chat with Mama and Auntie Libby. Mrs. Campbell, never wanting to miss anything, joined them. Jeannie watched Ella and Pearl race off along paths. Ella was quiet where Pearl was bubbly, but they were great friends.

"Well," Mrs. Campbell declared, "this lollygagging won't put jam on the table. Now, Priscilla," she ordered Jeannie's mother, "you sit right back down on that blanket. A woman in your condition! Your Jeannie will pick enough in no time, I'm sure."

Mama looked apologetically at her older daughter.

"I don't mind," Jeannie said. She found a bountiful patch and soon filled the last pail. She ran her hand through the depths of berries. They rolled back with a sound like a chuckle.

She breathed the heated-land smell as she meandered along the path. The Crowdis Barrens were covered in green, in soft breezes and cheerful voices, but the place would come into its name not many weeks from now. From the first bitter fall wind, the Barrens would be so empty and cruelly cold that no one would be able to believe there had ever been a day like this. And today, Jeannie couldn't believe in winter.

" 'Oh, Lord, I do fear,' " Mama recited at her as she returned, " 'Thou'st made the world too beautiful this year.' "

People threaded their way back to the wagons. They'd had enough berries and sun for one day. There were suppers to cook, blueberry preserves to make.

"Ella," Mama called to her little niece, "where's Pearl? Wasn't she with you?"

Ella looked around. "She was here a minute ago."

Mama shook her head. "That child!" she said, getting up carefully. "Jeannie, Pearl's wandered off again. Go get her, please."

Jeannie walked the narrow path between bushes and boulders to the last point she'd seen her sister.

"Pearl!" she called. She checked to see if her sister had reappeared in the crowd. People turned to watch expectantly, not yet alarmed.

Jeannie clambered onto a boulder. No sign of the child. An eagle cry sounded nearby, but Jeannie didn't look. The cry came again, then again. She turned.

From the highest heave of land, Cap Parker waved his arms at her. It was him whistling. *What does he want?* Jeannie wondered. She looked away to climb down, but another shrill whistle from Cap made her glance crossly back. He waved again, then pointed out behind the hill where he stood.

Jeannie strode forward, with the lowering sun in her eyes. As she came around the base of the hill, Pearl jumped out of the bushes. "BOO!" she shouted.

Jeannie staggered back. "Oh, you awful brat!"

Pearl laughed and laughed. "I scared ya! You thought I was the Bochdan, didn't you, Jeannie? *Ooh,* I'm the wicked spirit of the Margaree!"

Jeannie untangled herself from the blueberry bushes and grabbed Pearl's arm. "We should leave *you* here for the Bochdan to get you when the sun goes down!"

Pearl stamped her foot. "I was only playing," she insisted. "Anyway, Mama would never leave without me. I'm her baby."

"Not for long. The new baby will be here soon and you'll be nothing."

"You're mean!" Pearl cried, and pushed past her down the path.

"The Bochdan's coming for you, Pearl!" Jeannie called as she followed her back. "It wants you to be its baby now. *Ooh!*"

"You can't scare me," Pearl cried, and raced into the crowd around the wagons. "Mama, Mama, Jeannie's being mean to me! She says I won't be your baby anymore."

"Oh, Pearl," Mama said, "you can be my baby as long as you want, just stop wandering off like that. And, Jeannie, you be nice."

Pearl stuck out her tongue from around the edge of Mama's belly.

"Tattletale," Jeannie mouthed at her. She turned her back on Pearl and looked again to the hill. Cap was watching her – not Pearl, not the crowd around the wagons. She lifted her hand in a reluctant half-wave of thanks. He waved back, then ran down the far side.

Rev. Hope swung Pearl up onto the wide driver's seat of the wagon. When Jeannie climbed in the back, everyone shuffled over to make room and laughed when they bumped into each other. Tina was in the middle of wedding talk with Vivian Phillips, Sarah's older sister, who'd been in Tina's class at school. Jeannie stepped over feet and around children to settle in the only spot left, just behind the driver's seat, where Pearl perched as if she'd won a prize.

The wagon shook as the driver pulled himself up. "Hi, Cap Parker," Jeannie heard Pearl say. "Are you driving us this time?"

"Yup. Ready? Here we go!"

The horse lifted its great feet and started off.

Pearl interrogated Cap the whole way. How many brothers and sisters did he have? Three older brothers, no sisters, but he did have a girl cousin who was staying with them. Her name was Moira. No, Moira couldn't come today. Yes, he would tell his cousin about her, if Pearl wanted him to. No, he hadn't known Pearl was going to be a big sister soon. No, Jeannie hadn't told him.

"I don't have any brothers yet, just a big sister," Pearl informed him. "Are your big brothers mean to you?" Jeannie could tell from the voice that Pearl had turned to look back at her own sister.

Cap laughed. "They sure are," he said. "They call me pip-squeak, though I've told them not to. They're so mean, they have meetings to plan how to be meaner to me next time."

"Really?" Pearl was shocked. "Even Jeannie isn't that bad. But she yelled at me just 'cause I went in her room and decorated her mirror. I was only wanting to make it pretty."

"Well," Cap reasoned, "you wouldn't want her to mess with your things, would you?"

"No-o-o."

"Besides, you're lucky to have your own room. I have to share mine with all my brothers since we came to Gran's."

"You have to share? With all of them?"

"Sure do. And, boy, are they messy! One time they lost me for two days, I was so far behind all the boxes of junk they collect. Of course, I never make a mess, myself."

Jeannie couldn't help smiling.

"Tell me more," Pearl demanded.

"They're so messy, our mother had to buy a new set of dishes because her old ones all ended up in their rooms. Said she wasn't going in there for all the tea in China."

"Oh, that's not true! Tell me another one."

"Okay. They're so-o-o messy, my next oldest brother – that's Tam – didn't realize for a week he was sleeping on his pile of dirty clothes instead of his bed." Pearl laughed and laughed at Cap's jokes and talked at him the whole way.

Pearl's not so bad, Jeannie admitted to herself as the wagon bumped along and the low sun dazzled their eyes. Rev. Hope started the singing with "Blessed Be the Tie That Binds," and followed it with "She'll Be Coming Round the Mountain When She Comes." Jeannie drifted into half-dreams of a houseful of boys who were all Cap Parker. Everything they said got funnier and funnier. She jerked awake when the horse stopped.

"That's very kind of you, Cap," her mother was saying. They were right beside their own land, with only the field path left before they were home. The other wagon was nowhere in sight. Cap must have come around by the old lane, to bring them this close.

He hopped down to help Mama. He lifted Pearl and swung her in a circle before setting her on the ground. Jeannie stumbled groggily to the end of the wagon. She jumped, ignoring Cap's offer of help.

But, after all, he was the one who'd found Pearl before Mama had to worry. And he'd been kind to her sister all the way home. Jeannie made herself look right at him.

"Thank you," she pronounced formally. "You were really nice to Pearl."

"That's okay," he said. "She's fun to talk to, at least. I wish I had a kid sister or brother, instead of being the pip-squeak of the family."

"Believe me, her shine sort of wears off from rubbing me the wrong way every day."

Cap laughed. "That's funny!" He swung back up onto the wagon seat. "See you in school, Jeannie. Bye, Mrs. Shaw. Bye, pip-squeak."

The wagon moved on, everyone waving and calling good-bye. Jeannie took two pails, Mama took the others, and Pearl carried the picnic things. They trudged along the path through the high grass.

Pearl chattered the whole way, telling Mama everything Cap had said. "And he has to share his room with all his brothers," she added.

"You must have heard wrong, Pearl," Mama said. "Mrs. Parker's house is a big old place. There's plenty of room."

"No, Mama," Jeannie said. "I heard him, too."

"Oh, well," said Mama. "It's none of my business."

They struggled home. The whole way, the thought kept skipping around Jeannie's mind: *no one ever thought I was funny before. Everyone says Pearl's funny. But no one ever said it about me. How about that?*

68

CHAPTER

6

"Now I'm sorry we picked so many yesterday," Jeannie complained. They'd made jam all last evening and had kept at it after Sunday dinner today.

"Almost done." Mama lifted another rack of jam jars from the canning pot. "We'll leave one last bowlful to have fresh with cream again."

Jeannie took a glass of water out to the veranda. She had just settled on the step next to Lady when a streak of gray and white hurtled past. Pearl came next, calling, "Barncat, come to Pearlie! Jeannie, did you see Barncat? He wants to get ready for my tea party. Ella's coming, too, after she changes out of her Sunday dress."

"Maybe he's in the barn," Jeannie answered, giving the wrong direction on purpose.

Pearl shifted course. "Barncat, where are you? Let me make you pretty."

"Poor Barncat," Jeannie said. She went in to get changed for the walk to the post office that Mrs. MacDonald ran from her front hall. Every summer Mama sent for the same kind of shoes for school – sturdy brown loafers and thin white sneakers. This year Daddy had said, "Get that girl some nice shoes for her birthday, Priscilla. I'll have my next pay by the time they get here." Jeannie had studied the Eaton's catalogue for days, and had changed her order three times. Now the shoes had arrived.

Maybe I should take Pearl with me, Jeannie thought. She stepped back outside before she could change her mind. "Pearl?" she called, but got no answer.

"Is she gone again already?" Mama asked. "That child needs sandbags on her ankles to slow her down. What did you want her for, anyway?"

"Mr. MacDonald told Daddy at church that my shoes arrived. He said I could get them today, even though it's Sunday. I thought I'd let the pip-squeak tag along."

Mama stopped wiping the table to look at her. "That's so nice. 'For there is no friend like a sister in calm or stormy weather,'" she quoted.

Jeannie felt a small bruise of guilt. She'd decided to be nicer only after Cap Parker had been so kind to Pearl. *If he can do it,* she figured, *so can I.*

From the landing window on her way upstairs, she saw Pearl chase Barncat across the yard. Jeannie laughed at the strip of yellow dangling from the cat's scruffy neck. *Pearl must've caught Barncat at least once.*

Jeannie watched as the cat dodged, but Pearl got her pudgy grip on him. She sat down in the grass with Barncat in her lap. Pearl loved to dress the homely old cat in doll clothes, or swaddle him in a blanket and parade him in the doll carriage until Barncat would wrestle free to be caught again another day.

Pearl kept the cat in a stranglehold and tied a strip of red around his belly. She reached into the deep pocket of her sundress and pulled out a blue strip this time. She tied that one around a paw.

Jeannie was about to call Mama to come see how funny this was when she stopped laughing and started frowning. Those colors . . . looked awfully familiar. Pearl let go of Barncat to use both hands tying a bow. Barncat was out of her lap and into the barn before Pearl was on her feet. And from Pearl's pocket, as she ran, colored ribbons trailed.

"*Ooh,* I'm going to strangle her!" Jeannie ran to her room. Sure enough, her ribbons were gone. She stormed down and headed for the door.

"What's going on, Jeannie?" Mama asked.

"Pearl's taken all my ribbons again! She's going to get it this time!"

Mama stepped in front of her. "I want you to calm down first. I won't have my girls fighting like cats."

71

"Why don't you tell Pearl that?"

"I will. But you're older. We expect more patience from you."

"Patience! How can anyone be patient with that –"

"Enough, Jeannie!" Mama snapped. Jeannie took a deep breath and tried hard to cool down. "Now," said Mama, "when you find Pearl, just tell her I want her, understand?"

"Yes, Mama."

As Jeannie slapped open the screen door, Mama reached for her hand. "Dear," she said, "it's not that you're wrong. But, like the Bible says, 'Be not righteous overmuch.'"

What's wrong with being right? With her jaw clenched, Jeannie slipped her hand from under her mother's and crossed the yard.

"Pearl!" she called into the barn shadows. "Mama wants you. Right now!" No answer, no sound at all. She called again.

A rustle in the loft, and a trickle of hay drifted down.

"Ha!" Jeannie cried and ran for the ladder. "You just wait, Pearl Shaw!" She popped her head above the loft floor. All she saw was heaps of loose hay.

"Are you there, Pearl?" she whispered. Another rustle, then stillness. "Come out, come out, wherever you are, you little brat!" She climbed into the loft and tiptoed forward. As she passed the small window, Jeannie saw their little cousin Ella skip into the yard, calling out to Pearl.

72

Who's she talking to? Jeannie wondered. *Pearl's up here.*

Jeannie leaned out. She saw the unmistakable honey-colored hair directly below the window. *Pearl!*

"I could spit right on her head from here, if I weren't a girl," Jeannie muttered. She got ready to yell, but stopped. "If Pearl is down . . . there, what's behind . . . me?"

She spun around. Her heartbeat thundered. *Please, not a rat! I hate rats!*

Something moved in the hay between her and the ladder. Past the ladder now, coming closer. *There!* A flash of red, and gone again. *Is it bleeding?*

Jeannie pressed against the wall. She could feel a nail head digging into her back. Another flash of color, blue this time, then yellow. Jeannie screeched. A rainbow jumble of cat and hay came rolling right up to her feet. Barncat tumbled out, spitting, biting at all the ribbons tied in lumpy bows, with tufts of fur poking out between. He cried, twisted, tried to slip, bite, and scratch them off.

Jeannie dove for the hapless cat. "Those are *my* ribbons!" she yelled. Barncat jumped straight up at the sudden shout. He came down too near the open edge, scrabbled for a hold, and lost. Jeannie leaned forward in time to see him unscramble himself from the deep hay on the barn floor. He sneezed and was gone before she had swung a foot over the top of the ladder. Another couple of half-shredded ribbons lay in the yard. A yowl from under the veranda.

Jeannie crouched down. "C'mon, Barncat, let me help. Here, Puss-puss."

Mama appeared at the door, drying her hands. "What's going on now? Where's Pearl?"

"Somewhere around here," Jeannie said. "You should see what she did with my ribbons this time."

"Jeannie, please don't get upset if Pearl's wearing your ribbons. What harm can she do them? This time I'll make sure she realizes they're not for her."

"Make sure you tell her," Jeannie suggested, with her head halfway under the steps, "that they're not for the cow or the horse, either."

"Don't be silly –" Mama began, coming outside. At the creak of the screen door, Barncat shot from under the veranda, over Lady's head, and into the house. "What was that?" Mama cried.

"Oh, that was just Barncat. Here Barncat," Jeannie urged. "C'mon, old boy."

Barncat chased himself among the chair legs. His teeth hooked into the blue ribbon and he tipped over, still gnawing at it.

"Barncat, don't!" Jeannie cried. "That's a new one!"

She caught hold of an end. As the cat struggled, the bow came undone. Barncat raced out again, past Mama in the doorway. He leapt from the top step and started rolling, then dragged his belly over the grass. He was almost at the well when Jeannie came out again.

"Oh, no!" she shouted and began to run.

"Oh, dear," Mama sighed.

Even in this dry weather, the remains of a puddle surrounded the well. Barncat had crawled blindly into it by the time Jeannie caught up. He flipped himself over when she tried to grab him, soaking them both.

Mud flew everywhere. Barncat streaked between Jeannie's legs, muddying her from knees to ankles. Jeannie's mouth hung open. She held her arms out and looked from her legs up to her dress. She wiped at her splattered face.

"Oh, dear," Mama said once more.

The rosebushes shook violently and a pitiful howl emerged. Jeannie peered into the dappled shadows. "Come out, you silly old fella."

"*Ow!*" That was when her hair hooked in the rosebush, but she got a grip on loops of ribbon.

"*Yeowl!*" That was Barncat being dragged out fighting.

"Sorry, Barncat." Jeannie pinned him down and untied the ribbons. As the last one came loose, she let go. Barncat leapt away to hide under the stone foundation of the barn. He stayed there, howling insults.

Jeannie sat with the muddied, shredded ribbons around her.

Mama came down the steps.

"Don't!" Jeannie cried. "Just . . . leave me alone."

"Oh, Jeannie," Mama said softly.

"No. Don't say anything, unless it's to Pearl. Look at these!" She held up a mess of ribbons.

"Now, Jeannie. You know Pearl never meant this to happen."

"WHY?" Jeannie yelled. "Why do you always have to forgive her, no matter what?"

"I'm cross with her, too," Mama said, "but she's only four. She didn't do it to be mean. Just calm down a bit before I go get her."

"NO! She's a brat and . . . and I hate her. I HATE HER!" It exploded out of her.

Mama's hand flew to her mouth.

Jeannie jumped up and ran.

*J*eannie ran beyond the barn, into the woods – ran until she got to the stream.

She sat on her rock with her knees up and rested her hot forehead on crossed arms, her heart and head thudding. She pressed her hands against her ears, but couldn't escape from the words that echoed in her mind. They were, she knew, about the worst thing she could have said.

All alone in the middle of the forest, Jeannie argued, sobbed, talked herself through it and out the other side, until her anger began to shrivel. She'd put herself in the wrong again. *How'd this happen? I was going to be nicer to Pearl.* She shook her head over and over. Nothing her sister could do was bad enough for hate. She didn't need her mother here to tell her that.

How can I expect Mama to forgive me for this? The questions banged around until her head ached.

Finally she picked herself up and climbed down. She walked beside the stream, stepping gingerly over roots, holding on to tree trunks as she made her way home. She felt like someone recovering from the flu – shaky, worn a bit thin.

Through the porch screen, she saw Pearl on the stool at the sink, wearing a long apron, scrubbing ribbons on the washboard in a pan of soapy water, and quietly sobbing. Their mother stood nearby, talking to Pearl in a murmur. Mama saw Jeannie, kissed Pearl on the head, and came outside.

Jeannie couldn't look at her. Her throat was tight and sore. "I'm sorry. I never meant it."

"Hush," Mama said. "I know that." She nudged the dog with her foot. "Move over, old Lady." She and Jeannie sat on the step together. "I sent Ella home for a bit," Mama said. "You know, when Libby and I were little, we didn't get along, though we were only a year apart."

"But you're best friends."

"Now we are. Not then. Always bickering. More than once, we got a whipping for it, too."

"What did you fight about?"

"Don't remember, mostly."

"Did she take your things?"

"All the time. But I took hers, too. And I broke her mother-of-pearl brush. I think I did it . . . almost on purpose." Mama shook her head. "See? Even now, I can barely admit it. But after all these years, I finally know why I did it."

Jeannie couldn't imagine anything awful enough to make her patient mother do such a thing.

"Because," Mama said, "Libby could play the piano."

"What?"

"She played well. Nothing astounding, just prettily. But I had absolutely no music in these hands. 'Envy's a coal comes hissing hot from hell.' Isn't that good? I read it the other day. Don't tell your grandmother I said 'hell.' Anyway, it made me so cross that Libby should have this talent and not me. Oh, I know that's not why you're cross with Pearl. Barncat has more music in him than Pearl does. She's full of mischief," Mama went on. "Even I'm worn out with her. And she will be punished, but, Jeannie, she's only four. Don't you think that counts for something?"

"I guess so. Mama, I didn't buy one treat with my blueberry money, not one! Except those ribbons. And there is no way I'm letting Pearl have them! I'll hide them. But I'll be nicer to her, I promise."

"Well, you can start right now. I gave her such a talking to, she's in there crying. Made it sound real sad, the way she'd hurt her poor sister's feelings and all."

Jeannie went in alone. Pearl was hiccuping quietly now, squishing the ribbons to make the bubbles froth.

When she saw her sister, she started in crying again. "Oh, Jeannie, I'm so sorry . . . I broke . . . your heart!" She put sudsy fists to her eyes, then cried about the soap, too.

"Here, silly." Jeannie wiped Pearl's eyes with a corner of apron. "You didn't break my heart. You just ruined my ribbons."

"Yes, I did. I'm a bad sister."

"No, you're not. I'm the bad one."

"No, I am."

"Will you shut up, Pearl? I shouldn't have –"

"*Ooh,* I'm telling! You said 'shut up.'"

"You make me so mad sometimes! All right, I won't say it anymore. Let's try being friends."

Pearl scrunched up her nose. "We can't be friends. We're sisters."

"Can, too. What about Mama and Auntie Libby? They're friends."

"That's not the same. They're old."

"Would you quit arguing for once? Look, I'm going to the post office to pick up my birthday shoes. Do you want to come with me or not?"

"Yippee!" cried Pearl immediately. She swiped soapy hands down the apron. "I'll tell Mama." Halfway across the kitchen she turned back. "Can Ella come, too?"

"No. Ella's gone home."

"I could go get her real fast."

"No, I said!"

Pearl thought about it. "All right, then. I guess we need practice being friends, anyway." She ran to find Mama.

Jeannie trailed her hand through the suds. The moment Pearl had mentioned Ella, she had felt the anger again.

It's not that I don't like Ella. She's my cousin, after all. And Pearl and Ella have played together since they were babies. Jeannie stopped. *Am I jealous? Pearl has never, ever been without her best friend.*

"I am," she admitted aloud. "I'm jealous."

Mama came in with Pearl skipping ahead of her. "Jeannie," Mama said, "are you sure you feel up to taking Pearl with you after all?"

No, not really, Jeannie thought, but out loud she said, "We'll be fine, Mama."

Pearl hopped along the road. She threw stones at the creek bed below, shouting, "Look how far I can throw, Jeannie! I'll get it in the water this time. Look, Jeannie!"

Jeannie wished her sister would be quiet for once. She swallowed her frustration. *Pearl's right. Being good sisters takes lots of practice. Mama and Auntie Libby always like being together, when they're working or having a pot of tea. Will we ever be like that?* Jeannie wondered. She studied Pearl, who was flicking a stick at pebbles on the shoulder of the road. Dirt flew.

"Hey! Watch out with that stick," Jeannie squawked, backing up.

"Young ladies don't say 'hey,'" Pearl lectured her. Then she recited in a singsong voice, "'Hay is for horses, better for cows. Pigs would eat it if they knew how.'" They'd heard it often enough from their mother.

Pearl continued to trail the stick through the dust. As Jeannie passed her again, she waved it in the air. "I'm your fairy godmother," she pronounced. "You can make three wishes, Jeannie Shaw."

Jeannie was about to ignore her when she thought of her promise to be nicer. She tipped her head sideways. "What should I wish for? Do I have to wish them out loud?"

"How'm I supposed to grant wishes if I can't hear them, silly?"

Jeannie rolled her eyes. "All right. *Hmm* . . . I wish I had a best friend. I wish I had a hundred dollars. And, oh, I don't know . . . I wish I didn't have to walk all the way to the post office. I'm so hot! C'mon, slowpoke."

The sound of a vehicle made them shift to the shoulder of the road. It was the doctor's car, big and new and black, one of the few cars in the valley. The loud horn beeped a greeting and the girls waved. Jeannie's hand froze in midair. She spun in place to follow the car as it rumbled past in a cloud of dust. There was a passenger in the car, besides the doctor's wife who waved from the front seat. Barely visible in the shadows of the rear window, a pale young face stared back at Jeannie for a second before turning abruptly away.

"Who was that?" Jeannie gasped. The car had already disappeared around a bend.

"The doctor, stupid," Pearl said, rubbing her eyes from the dust.

"No! There was someone with him! Not just his wife. A girl, in the backseat!"

"I didn't see anybody. Maybe it's their daughter."

"Pearl, you know perfectly well Dr. Andrews doesn't have any children."

"They coulda kept her a secret. Their house is real big."

"Don't be stupid," Jeannie snapped. She tried to follow the car in her mind. *Probably heading to Inverness. Who could it be? Whoever it is, will she be coming back? How can I find out?*

But she couldn't concentrate with Pearl chattering, "... or maybe they're adopting her, or keeping her prisoner."

Jeannie huffed with impatience. "Pearl, be quiet! I know, I'll ask Mrs. MacDonald when we get to the post office. C'mon, slowpoke!"

"In a minute." Pearl was digging at another clod of earth. She swatted at a wasp. Then she hummed a song and raised the stick to flick at another wasp.

"Don't slap at them," Jeannie said, "and they'll leave you alone."

"*Ow!*" cried Pearl. "It *didn't* leave me alone. It stung me!" She dropped the stick. More wasps circled, rising from the ground.

"Wasps! Pearl, get away from there. It's a mud-wasp nest!"

"HELP!" Pearl screamed and swatted. Wasps surrounded her.

"Run, Pearl!" But the child was in too much panic to do more than writhe and dodge. Jeannie grabbed her sister's hand. She headed pell-mell down the bank to the stream, covering Pearl as much as she could.

"Oh, *ow!*" Jeannie felt a sting on her own neck, another on her shoulder, but had no hand free to protect herself as she hugged Pearl to her. She stumbled to the middle and pushed Pearl into the shallow water, sat down herself – sandals, socks, and all – and splashed wildly around their heads. Pearl, crying and choking, did the same. They both screamed as they sprayed water everywhere.

After a frantic minute, Jeannie finally dared to look. Pearl kept swinging until Jeannie grabbed her arms, causing Pearl to screech again.

"They're gone, Pearl. Stop!"

Pearl opened her eyes. They checked their backs to make sure the wasps were all gone. Pearl had five stings on her arms, more than that on her legs. Jeannie had several herself.

Pearl sobbed. "They hurt, Jeannie!"

"Lie back in the water. It'll cool them a bit."

"What if those wasps come back?"

"They won't. Anyway, they were defending themselves. You attacked their home, you know."

"They're still bad, bad, bad!" Pearl insisted, pounding the water. She stopped and cried harder. "My stings hurt too much," she whimpered and cradled both arms at once.

"Let's put mud on them," Jeannie told her. "That's what Mama does." She dolloped cool mud onto her sister's stings, then her own.

Pearl sniffled while she watched. "Mama won't spank us for getting muddy, 'cause this is like medicine, right? Jeannie, do you put honey on bee stings?"

"What?"

"You put mud on mud-wasp stings. Wouldn't you put honey on honeybee stings?"

"I don't know, Pearl. You're funny."

"I don't feel funny. I feel bad. My head hurts."

"Let me see. Oh, gosh!" There were more stings under the hair, and a huge lump rising above her sister's eye. "We better get you home."

They started back along the road. Pearl looked awful, with water dripping and streaks of mud down her arms and legs. Her stings were red lumps and her eye was swelling shut.

"Poor Pearlie," Jeannie said. Her own stings throbbed, but she kept an arm around her sister's shoulders. *She's only little, after all,* Jeannie thought.

Pearl wobbled along, out of step with Jeannie, going slower until her shoes barely scuffed through the dust.

How can I get Pearl home? No one's passed since the doctor's car. "Here," Jeannie said. She crouched and gave her sister a piggyback. Pearl lay limply against her as Jeannie struggled home. "Almost there," she said at every bend, to convince herself as much as Pearl.

"Never going to be a fairy godmother again," Pearl mumbled.

Jeannie stopped in the road to catch her breath. "What, Pearl? You're not making sense."

"Got your wish," Pearl managed. "Don't have to walk to the post office after all. Not getting the other two. Wishes hurt too much."

"Let's get home," Jeannie said, and started walking again.

8

M ama was picking runner beans when the girls got home. Jeannie's legs wobbled as she bent to ease Pearl from her back. She couldn't have carried her another step.

Mama took Pearl's swollen face carefully in her hands. "Child," she said, "what's happened to you?" Pearl bent over and threw up.

"Wasps," Jeannie told her mother. "She was stung maybe twenty times."

Pearl started to cry again. "Come on, honey," Mama said. With Jeannie on the other side, they walked Pearl up the steps and laid her on the kitchen couch. Jeannie wrung out a dish towel at the sink pump and gave it to her mother to lay on Pearl's forehead.

Mama shook her head as she examined Pearl's stings. The bump over her eye was now as big as an egg. "So many of them," Mama said. "Jeannie, run to Phillips' Garage and phone the doctor."

Exhausted as she was, Jeannie started for the door, then skidded to a halt. "But we saw him, on the way to the post office," she told Mama. "He was heading towards Inverness, I guess. And his wife was with him, and . . . someone else, but I never saw her before. She looked –"

"Hush, Jeannie. Let me think. When you pick up the phone, Mrs. MacDonald will come on the line at the post office. Tell her what's happened and that we need to find the doctor. She'll know what to do. Hurry!"

Jeannie ran all the way. The sun pounded in her head and seemed to flash halos of hot light. Mr. Phillips was nowhere in sight when she got to the garage. Jeannie lifted the receiver off the wall and turned the crank.

"Who do you wish to call?" came the tinny voice at the other end.

"Mrs. MacDonald, it's Jeannie Shaw! Pearl's been stung a whole lot and Mama says could you please find the doctor. We saw his car heading for Inverness a while ago. . . . Uh-huh. I'll tell her. Bye."

Jeannie had to will her feet to keep moving all the way back. Auntie Libby called out from her front door as Jeannie passed, to ask what was going on, then grabbed Ella's hand and came, too.

Mama had wiped most of the mud off Pearl and was

draping cool cloths over her to bring her temperature down. She dabbed vinegar on the stings and made a gauze bag filled with wet tea, to lay on the swollen eye.

"All we can do now," Mama said, "is wait for the doctor."

Auntie Libby started trimming the pail of beans Mama had picked. Ella curled up at the other end of the couch and soon fell asleep. Mama sat beside Pearl and kept replacing the cool cloths. All was quiet except for the snap of the beans and Pearl's moans.

Jeannie sat at the kitchen table. She tried to think about the girl she'd seen in the car. *I can't wait to ask Dr. Andrews who she is. I'll. . . .*

The thought trailed off. She couldn't think straight. The walls were acting funny, too, pulsing in and out as if they were breathing with her. Jeannie put her head down on her arm on the table.

Ages later, it seemed, the doctor's car pulled into the driveway and Auntie Libby jumped up to let him in. Dr. Andrews examined Pearl and took her temperature.

"A few more," Jeannie heard him say, "and she might have been in serious trouble. Not to worry. Her fever's mild. You've done all the right things."

His voice seemed to Jeannie to come from far away. She struggled to focus. *Wasn't there something I wanted to ask,* she wondered, *something about a car? That's silly, we don't have a car.* She stood up and immediately felt worse. "I got stung, too," she tried to say, but she must have only thought it, not spoken aloud, because no one took any notice of her. *So stuffy in here. Maybe if I go outside.*

While Mama was listening to the doctor and Auntie Libby was making him a cup of tea, Jeannie headed for the door. *Why does it keep moving away like that?* The sun slammed at her when she made it to the veranda and set her head pounding harder. She reached out to steady herself and felt the hot scratch of the shingles.

She leaned forward, when she sat down in her mother's rocker, until she was folded almost double, and waited for the dizziness to pass. Her head felt as heavy as a stone as she lifted it in slow motion. The whole yard quivered in the heat. She squinted her eyes against the glare.

Jeannie tipped her head and tried to look out of only one eye. It was less painful. Something big and black and shiny beside the barn. She forced her eyes open a little more.

A car. The doctor's car, she remembered that much. *Why is he here? Because I'm sick. No, not me. It's Pearl.*

There was something awfully important about this car, something she'd meant to ask the doctor. Jeannie peered at it, parked beneath the biggest maple tree. The giant chrome grille shot fireworks of light at her. The car itself was shadowed inside, the interior almost as big as their porch. But something moved in the front seat. Someone.

Jeannie sucked in her breath as it came to her. The girl she'd seen earlier. The girl was here, at Jeannie's own home! She pushed herself up by the arms of the rocker.

I'm going to meet her after all!

She made it down the first step, concentrating on the face that was staring out at her now from the car window. The blonde hair glowed like gold in the sun. The head shook, as if saying *no* to something.

Jeannie made to go down the next step, but her legs wobbled and, light as a dandelion puff, her body drifted into the parched grass.

"Help!" she heard a voice call. "Somebody help that girl!" A car horn blasted. *Beep! Beep!*

Stop it! Jeannie's aching mind demanded. She dragged a hand up to cover her ear. *Who's doing that? Oh, I know, that's Cecilia. That's my friend Cecilia.*

Lady had left her shady spot for once and shuffled her arthritic legs down the steps. She stood over Jeannie, whining and licking her face.

"Go away, Lady," Jeannie mumbled. "Have to get up now. Cecilia's come to meet me and. . . ."

Next thing, she was being carried into the lovely darkness of the house and laid on the living room sofa.

"Poor thing," she heard her mother say, "I should have seen she wasn't herself. Jeannie, dear, can you hear me?"

"She'll be right as rain in a few minutes, Mrs. Shaw." That was the doctor talking. "More sun and stress than wasp stings. Sweetened tea is the medicine for her now. Well, I must be going. I have a patient to get home."

"Thank you so much, Dr. Andrews. Bye now. . . . Yes, I'll call and let you know how they are."

Heavy feet strode across the floor. The door opened and clicked shut. After a moment, Jeannie heard a car start. The chug of the engine faded down their drive and was gone.

CHAPTER

9

Auntie Libby brought Jeannie her tin mug with a spoon in it. Jeannie sipped and made a face. "It's so sweet!"

"That's what the doctor ordered. Drink it up, dear."

Jeannie shuddered but kept drinking. Her head stopped spinning by the time she finished it. She got up carefully and returned to the kitchen. *Pearl has stopped crying, at least. Her lumps and bumps look terrible!*

"Priscilla, we're going now," Auntie Libby was saying in the porch. "After I get Murdoch his supper, I'll be back to see how you're doing."

"Thanks for everything, Libby," Mama said. "What would I do without you?" She caught sight of Jeannie when she came back into the kitchen. "Oh, here's my poor girl. You look a lot better. I thought I'd faint, myself, when I came out and saw you lying there."

"Who was the girl, Mama?" Jeannie asked.

"What's that, dear? Oh, the girl in the car? I don't know. I was so worried about Pearl and then about you, I didn't think to ask. Dr. Andrews didn't say, either." Mama held Pearl's tin cup under the child's chin, helping her take sips. "Don't drink too much, Pearl, until your tummy settles."

Jeannie wandered back out to the yard. In the shade of the big tree, she stood in the crushed grass where the doctor's car had been.

As the sun went down, so did Pearl's temperature. She was sitting up by the time Daddy arrived with the block of ice he'd gone to fetch from the ice house Dougald MacFarlane's family kept. Mama fashioned an ice pack to lay on Pearl's head, and let her have her tin cup full of ice chips to suck on.

After supper, Ella was allowed to return for a few minutes with Auntie Libby, and Pearl told the story all over again while everyone had a treat of ice chips.

"Then," she said, "Jeannie fought off millions of giant wasps and saved me!"

"You're delirious again," Jeannie said, but she liked to hear Pearl tell it.

The next morning, while Jeannie was getting ready for school, Mama helped Pearl downstairs. Daddy arrived, whispered to Pearl, and slipped a small package into her hands before heading back to work. The swelling over her eye had gone down and she was feeling better, still enjoying all the attention.

Queen of the show again, Jeannie thought.

Pearl peeked in the paper bag and smiled. "Jeannie," she said, "come here."

"If you think I'm going to wait on you, Princess Pearl, you've got another think coming. I have to leave for school."

"No, silly. Here! These are for you."

Jeannie shot a questioning look at her mother. Mama just lifted her eyebrows.

"Look inside!" Pearl bossed.

Jeannie opened the paper bag as if a mouse might hop out. She pulled out three new ribbons – a ruby red, an emerald green, and a rich sapphire blue.

"I'm sorry I messed up your ribbons," Pearl began, "but it was really Barncat who –"

"Pearl," Mama warned.

"Well, you know. You said they weren't for decorating Daddy. You didn't say anything about – oh, all right," Pearl went on, seeing Mama's expression, "I won't take them ever, ever again. And please don't be mad about it anymore." Her face crumpled in the drama of her apology and she sobbed out, "I only wanted to make Barncat pretty for once!"

Jeannie rolled her eyes. Mama shook her head and went into the pantry.

"I bought those ribbons," Jeannie said, "to make *me* pretty for once. But thanks. These are really nice."

"That's stupid! You're the prettiest girl in the valley."

"No, I'm not. Verity Campbell is, and she knows it."

"Well, you're the prettiest girl your age in the valley, then."

"Pearl, I'm the *only* girl my age in the valley," Jeannie said as she grabbed her schoolbag. "Mama, I'm leaving now. And I won't be right home, remember. I still have to pick up my shoes and then get back to school for Glee Club practice."

When Jeannie got to the post office after school, Mrs. MacDonald was kneading bread dough. She had to wait until the post mistress shaped two loaves and a pan of rolls, and popped them in the oven. The whole time, Mrs. MacDonald talked. She asked after Pearl and shared all her remedies for stings and fevers. Jeannie finally escaped, clutching her parcel, and hurried to get back to school in time for practice. No time left to examine her lovely new shoes.

It wasn't until she neared the school that Jeannie realized she'd forgotten to ask about the mysterious girl in the doctor's car. She stamped her foot in frustration.

There was a whistle behind her, an eagle's call. She didn't turn. She'd already seen that it was Cap Parker coming along the road back to school. He'd joined the Glee Club, too.

She pretended not to hear him.

Ahead was the Three-Headed Monster. She was stuck with hurrying to catch up to the older girls, or having Cap catch up with her. She argued with herself again.

He found Pearl for me, didn't he? Yes, but he called me snooty at the Church Supper. Still, he was real nice to Pearl on the wagon ride home. Yes, but he's a dumb boy. He's not dumb. What about his essay on his father? Yes, but . . . he's . . . a boy!

"Wait!" she called. The girls turned and looked at her as if she were a stranger.

"Oh," said Verity Campbell. "It's you. What?"

Jeannie's face burned. "I'm going to Glee Club, too."

"We know that," Melanie Matthews said.

At least they hadn't turned their backs on her yet. She'd just have to die right there if they did. "Can I walk with you?" The girls looked at each other. Jeannie held out the parcel. "I just got my new shoes from Eaton's. They're black patent leather."

"*You* have new shoes?" Melanie repeated. "That aren't brown?"

Jeannie wouldn't give up. "Want to see them?"

"Sure," Verity decided for them all. "Show us when we get to school."

Jeannie caught up. A glance back showed Cap kicking a stone along the road as if he hadn't even noticed them.

Jeannie nodded while the girls talked. She laughed when they did. She skipped up the school steps just as jauntily – one of the girls. *This is what Verity must feel like all the time,* she thought.

"So," Verity demanded in the empty classroom, "show us these new shoes before Mousie gets here."

Her daring to use their teacher's nickname, right there in the school, made them all laugh. Even Jeannie giggled . . . just as Cap came in. He shot a look at her, like she was committing some crime.

Who does he think he is? Jeannie tried to flip her hair as Melanie was doing, but it didn't really work.

The girls crowded around as she unknotted the string on her brown-paper parcel. Even the shoe box was fancier than usual. And there was the perfect shine of her first black patent leather shoes.

"Silver buckles," noted Verity. "Pretty." The other girls nodded when Verity gave her seal of approval.

Jeannie beamed. Thank goodness she hadn't picked up her parcel yesterday. Maybe Pearl really had granted her wish for a friend. Three friends.

"*Hmph,*" sniffed Melanie. "Aren't you allowed to wear heels yet, Jeannie Shaw?"

"These have heels!" Jeannie retorted, grabbing a shoe and holding it upside down in Melanie's face.

"Of course they do," Verity soothed. "Jeannie's lucky. She's already tall enough without high heels. And she's only ten, after all."

"I'm twelve – almost! My birthday's next week, you know." Verity Campbell knew perfectly well how old she was. The Campbells knew everybody's business.

Verity and Sarah were checking who had arrived so far. Melanie was smoothing out her skirt. Jeannie racked her brain for something to keep their interest.

"*Umm,*" she began, "what's your middle name, Verity?"

Verity swung her head. Her hair spread around her shoulders like melting gold. "Tell yours first."

"It's Stephanie. Isn't that awful? It was my great-grandmother's."

"She should've kept it," Melanie said.

"*Shush,*" Verity scolded. "Stephanie's kind of a pretty name." Melanie fiercely patted at her skirt again, making sure to look bored. Verity ignored her and continued. "Mine's Amelia, after Amelia Earhart. Such a romantic life, being a lady pilot, getting lost forever like that."

"Liar!" snapped the wounded Melanie. "It's Martha and we all know it!"

"Well, I'm changing it," Verity insisted.

"You can't do that!" Melanie challenged. Melanie and Verity turned their backs on each other.

"You can have any name you want, really," Jeannie rushed in, before they all upped and left. "Amelia's a beautiful name."

Verity smiled at her. It felt wonderful.

Melanie was inspecting a pearl button on the cuff of her new white blouse. Her ankles were crossed and Jeannie peeked at her shoes. They didn't have any more heel than hers did, she noted.

"So," she tried, "what's your middle name, Melanie?"

"This is stupid. I don't want to play this game."

"If you don't want to say," Jeannie told her, "it doesn't matter."

"It's not that I don't want to. It's just silly."

"It's Mary," Verity cut in. "That's her middle name."

"Verity *Martha* Campbell," Melanie snapped, "I guess I can say my own name or not, without your help!" The two girls glared at each other.

For friends, Jeannie thought, *they sure are mean.*

She looked desperately to Sarah Phillips. Sarah gazed back, then said, "Mine's Dorothy. So boring. But if I got to change it, I'd choose Jessica. What would you choose, Jeannie Stephanie Shaw?"

"I never thought about it before," Jeannie said. "What

would be good?" The tension eased. Verity suggested the name Francesca. Sarah offered Bernadette. Jeannie was enjoying herself again. "I think maybe . . . Cecilia's a lovely name. Or maybe a short name would be better, sort of elegant – like Mary is."

Melanie turned to look at Jeannie. "I don't know," she finally offered, "Cecilia's not so bad. For a change. You get kind of tired of an elegant name like Mary."

Verity said, "I bet I know the middle name of everyone in this school. Dougald MacFarlane's is Angus. And his sister Beth, that just started, her name is Elizabeth Joan."

Verity rhymed off the full name of everyone in the room. "I even know hers," Verity whispered. Miss MacQueen bustled by on her way to the old piano, herding her most promising new singers from the junior class. "It's Penelope . . . Priscilla . . . MacQueen." The other girls laughed into their hands. Jeannie kept silent. Priscilla was her own mother's name.

"PeePee MacQueen!" Verity burst out. Even Jeannie joined in the explosion of muffled giggles.

Mr. Moss strode in. "Douglas Dexter Angus Moss," Verity pronounced. "Dexter was his mother's maiden name," she added importantly. Jeannie wasn't sure why such a name should be so funny but she, too, giggled behind her song sheet. It was hard to stop, just like laughing in church.

Boys and girls were looking sideways at them. Some grinned, wishing they were part of the group. Some frowned, in case they were the butt of the joke. Either way, Jeannie was enjoying being on the inside for a change.

Cap Parker didn't look their way at all.

Jeannie asked, "What's Cap's middle name, Verity? You missed him."

Verity squinched her eyes in thought. "I don't know," she admitted. "Let's ask him. Cap!" she called.

"No!" Jeannie yelped. Cap turned.

"What's your middle name, Cap?" Verity called.

He looked at her blankly, then shook his head. "Don't have one," he said, and returned to talking to the boys, but Jeannie saw the back of his neck turn red.

Verity shrugged. "He's just Chris, then. Christopher Parker."

"He does, too, have a middle name," Jeannie insisted. "Everybody does." She stood up. Cap glanced over, then quickly turned away again.

"Where are you going?" Sarah asked. "Glee Club's starting."

"I bet I can find out Mr. Cap Parker's mysterious name."

Verity eyed her as if she were slightly interesting again. "How?"

"The register."

"You wouldn't dare!" Verity said.

"I dare you!" said Melanie.

Jeannie raised her eyebrows and shot Melanie a look. She slipped out and sauntered along the hall between the two classrooms as if heading for the girls' privy out back. She ducked into the senior classroom through the rear door, lifting it so its old hinges wouldn't squeak, and scurried to the front of the room where Mousie had his desk. And the register.

Her heart was pounding. She'd never done such a thing in her entire life. *Do I dare?* But now that she'd said she would, there was no going back.

She pulled the heavy dictionary from the library shelf behind Mousie's desk. If anyone came in, she would pretend to be looking up their vocabulary words. She sat on the edge of the principal's chair and slid open the top desk drawer. *There it is! This won't take long.*

She tugged the drawer open farther. There was a handkerchief on top of the register, wrapped around something. Jeannie tugged on its corner to pull it aside. The handkerchief unfolded, revealing the grinning edge of a set of ivory-colored false teeth. If Mousie came in now, she didn't know what she'd do. In a singsong voice, she muttered, "Shut the *drawer* and get *out* of here," as she lifted the cover of the big white book. The very first page showed the master list for the whole school, written in Mousie's precise script.

"Andrews, Campbell, Donaldson," she read down the page. "Kirkpatrick, MacFarlane, MacFarlane, McLean, MacDonald, MacDonald, MacDonald, Matthews, O'Sullivan, Parker . . . there it is!"

She studied Mousie's tiny writing, expecting to see "Christopher," but that wasn't it. That definitely wasn't it.

Even as she absorbed the information, she was distracted by the entry directly beneath Cap's. A double line had been ruled through it. She peered at the crossed-out name, trying to decipher it. She was pretty sure the last name was Phalen, but the inked lines almost blotted out the first name. E . . . s . . . *Estelle? Esther?*

Who can that be? I thought I knew all the little ones who just started. Did I miss one? She frowned. *Maybe it's Cap's little cousin, the one who doesn't start until next year. What was the name he'd told Pearl on the wagon ride?*

Someone's coming! Jeannie flipped the book shut with a bang. The footsteps stopped. She slid the desk drawer closed, winced as it squeaked. As the drawer clicked shut, the classroom door opened. Cap Parker stood there.

"What are you doing in here?" he demanded. He eyed the desk as if he suspected the answer.

Jeannie bristled. *Who does he think he is – the teacher? Wait 'til I tell everyone that name of his!*

"Just discovering new names," she said, slowly and deliberately, as her heart pounded.

For a second, when she saw the look on his face, Jeannie was ashamed. *Even if it is Cap Parker, with the oddest name I've ever heard, what is the matter with me?*

"What's the matter with you, Jeannie Shaw?" Cap asked. "Just mind your own darn business!" He strode away, leaving the door to swing shut, crying on its hinges.

Jeannie shoved the dictionary onto its shelf and bolted from the room. By the time she slipped into her spot in the second row, Glee Club had begun. She'd been gone less than two minutes. Out of the corner of her eye, she caught sight of Cap in the back row. He was staring straight ahead without singing. *Is he going to tell on me? Well, I have something to tell first.*

Crispus . . . Aldershot . . . Parker. What a name! His secret was about to be announced to the gossipiest girls in the school.

Jeannie absently sang the song. As they finished, Verity tugged her sleeve. Jeannie shook her head, grinning to the girls. She didn't dare speak with Mousie right in front of them.

"Quiet, everyone, please!" Mr. Moss ordered. He sounded a note on the round pitch pipe to start the next song. *Of course! That's what Mousie meant on the first morning, when I heard him tell Cap he'd "keep that quiet for now." Why would Mousie be willing to hide it? Why would a boy like Cap care so much about a name, even such an odd one? But look how red he is again.*

It hit home that she now had Cap's mysterious, hilarious name in her hands.

As practice finished, Verity reached out and pinched Jeannie's arm.

"*Ow!*"

"Tell us," demanded Verity in a stage whisper, "before we simply die! What's his middle name?"

Melanie and Sarah joined in, crowding Jeannie into a corner. They were already giggling. What a laugh they'd all have when she told them it was Aldershot and that Cap's first name wasn't Christopher at all but ... Crispus!

Over their heads, Jeannie caught sight of Cap. He was looking right at her, all calm again. But she knew.

"For heaven's sake," Melanie exclaimed, "did you find out anything or not, stupid?"

Verity pinched her arm again.

"*Ow!* Stop that," Jeannie said. "Yes, he has a middle name." She looked at Cap looking at her. She pictured herself and these girls through his cool dark eyes.

"Angus," she said at last. "Cap's name is Christopher Angus Parker. *C, A, P* – Cap."

"Is that all?" Verity said, disgusted. "Every second boy in Inverness County is named Angus."

"You chickened out, didn't you, Jeannie Shaw?" Melanie shot at her.

"I did not! I saw his name. It's not my fault it wasn't interesting. And," Jeannie added for good measure, "I had to move Mousie's extra set of false teeth to get to the register."

"*Eww!*" cried Sarah. "I'm never touching that drawer."

Melanie said, "How could you do that? Don't touch us!"

Verity laughed, pushing Jeannie away.

They aren't being friends with me, she admitted to herself at last. She could hear it in their hard laughter. *They aren't even nice to each other. Why did I ever think I wanted to be friends with you three, anyway?* she wondered.

Cap was still watching. *He thinks I've just told them his stupid name. I don't care. Why should I care what he thinks?*

But she was mortified at being lumped with these airy-fairy girls. Jeannie pulled her arm from Verity's bossy grip. "Fine!" she said. She kept her back to the girls and busied herself with gathering up her Eaton's parcel.

"Well!" she heard Melanie exclaim in a huff as she walked out the door.

10

Halfway home, Jeannie heard running feet behind her.

"Wait up!" Cap called.

"Oh, great," she muttered. She sighed and stopped, not looking back. "Well?" she said, when he caught up.

"Did you tell those girls what you found out?" he demanded. "I really need to know."

"No. I didn't."

"So, are you going to?"

"No. I couldn't hand you over to them at the last minute," she admitted. "But it's bound to come out. Why hide a silly old name?"

"Essie wants it that way, not me! Look, you can't tell anyone about her."

"Essie? Who's . . .? You mean, the new name in the register? Who *is* she?"

"My other cousin," he muttered. "Essie Phalen."

"You have another cousin here? How old is she?"

"She's twelve, same as me. But I can't talk about her!"

"Twelve. Then it *was* her! She was in Dr. Andrews' car yesterday, wasn't she?" Jeannie asked. "But that's great! Why isn't she in school? When can I meet her?"

"You can't."

"Of course I can. We should have met yesterday, but, next thing, the doctor had taken her away. She'll *want* to meet me," she insisted. "We'll be friends."

Voices were approaching from beyond the last bend. Cap tugged Jeannie's arm. "C'mon. I don't want the whole school listening, especially not the Giggle Girls."

"Is that what you call them? I call them the Three-Headed Monster of the Margaree." Jeannie realized she was babbling as she let herself be hurried along. She felt like dancing down the road.

They passed Phillips' Garage, where Sarah Phillips might see them as she came home, and turned out of sight onto Jeannie's lane.

"No," Cap insisted, "Essie doesn't want to meet any-body! She'll kill me just for this."

Jeannie laughed. "You make her sound horrible."

"She is," Cap grumbled. "Ever since she got sick, she's been mad at the world."

"Sick?" Jeannie's stomach flipped. She didn't want to hear that anything was wrong, didn't want to guess. She put her hands up to ward it off.

"Polio," Cap said, barely above a whisper. "She had polio."

An icy wave washed over Jeannie. Polio had been terrifying the world for years. There were dozens of cases in Halifax, hundreds across the country, each summer.

"It's okay," Cap said. "She got it last year; she's not contagious. And Dr. Andrews checked us. None of us has it, honest."

Guilty relief swept most of her fear aside, but the chill remained.

"How bad?" she asked.

"Bad enough. She was in Yarmouth Hospital for months, in one of those iron lungs." He shuddered. "She's a lot better. It's only her leg that's paralyzed now. Gran says Essie could walk again if she'd just try. She says a conveyance man could drive Essie to school next year, but she has to snap out of it first."

They came to the wooden fence where Jeannie would climb over and cut across to her house. She laid her books on the post. She saw the ones Cap was carrying, two identical English Grammars among them.

"That's why you've been taking home extra books. . . ."

"Not that it does any good," Cap said. "She barely

looks at them, just sits there. She won't try to walk; she won't even go outside! She hates it here."

Jeannie hoisted herself to the top rail and sat. "Why is she here, then?"

He shrugged. "Their father came home from France with weak lungs that never cleared up. He died while Essie was sick, so she couldn't even go to the funeral. Then her mother had to take a job in Halifax to pay all the doctor bills."

Jeannie picked at a knothole in the post.

Cap was crouched down, pulling grass blades one after another as he talked. "I know she's been through awful stuff. So have lots of people! What about all the ones in those German concentration camps they talk about, people who lost their whole families? Anyway," he went on, "last spring, Gran wrote a letter asking us to come live with her. It would make life a lot easier on Mom, but she wrote back saying she couldn't because she was looking after her sister's kids. Gran said bring them, too. That made Mom cry, I tell ya."

He smiled for once. "Gran was a nurse, you know, until she got polio herself in one of the bad summers, but *she* got married and had kids, didn't she? Gran told Essie she should be walking with canes by now. Essie yelled at her to get out. Out of Gran's own house! Gran says Essie'll have to get over it, same as everyone else. Essie called her a heartless old cripple and said none of us was allowed to tell anyone she's here."

Crows cried in the trees and the dry wind sighed. Jeannie stared at the knothole the whole time.

It's not fair, she thought. *This isn't how it's supposed to work out. We're supposed to be friends, Essie Phalen and me.*

She climbed down on her side of the fence, barely aware of Cap.

"... so that's why," Cap was saying, "you can't meet her and you can't tell, okay? She's just being a stupid girl, but Mom says we have to try it Essie's way for now."

"I won't tell them at school," said Jeannie. "I promise."

Cap took a deep breath in relief. "That's great! Well, I'd better go. See you tomorrow, Jeannie."

He shifted the books under his arm and headed back down the road. When he turned at the bend and saw that Jeannie was still there, he waved and called, "Thanks!"

11

"Thanks," Jeannie said to her parents at supper. "I knew you'd understand."

Mama shook her head. "That poor family. We had no idea. There must be something we can do for them."

Jeannie perked right up. "Well, you know," she began, "Moira's the same age as Pearl and Ella. I was thinking...."

An hour later, Daddy was driving down the narrow road to old Mrs. Parker's place. Jeannie balanced one of Mama's blueberry pies, still warm from the oven. Pearl and Ella, in the middle, clutched their own dolls in one arm. Pearl had an old doll of Jeannie's in the other. Pearl's wasp stings looked no worse than large mosquito bites now. As soon as she'd heard about this new little girl, Moira, she had begged Mama to let her and Ella go see her, swearing she was suddenly feeling much better.

Jeannie's stomach fluttered. *Cap's only a stupid boy; he doesn't know about these things. Essie was just upset when she said she didn't want to meet anyone. She'll be real glad for us to be friends. I'll treat her just like she's normal. We'll visit and she'll wish I didn't have to leave so soon. But I'll promise to have Daddy drive me back on Saturday. Then we'll spend the whole day talking and getting her started on her schoolwork. Won't Mousie be surprised? Won't Cap?*

And, yet, Jeannie's stomach was more nervous the closer they got. "*Umm . . .* Daddy?" she said over Pearl's and Ella's heads. "Let's just have the girls meet Moira, all right? Let's not say anything about you-know-who for now." Daddy scratched his head. "Cap says Essie's shy," she explained, "about meeting people and stuff."

That much was true. There was no way she was going to admit what Cap had really said. She hadn't broken her word. She'd promised Cap she wouldn't tell anyone at school. And she didn't lie to her parents. She just didn't tell them a couple of things. *Boys don't know everything,* she reminded herself.

The truck struggled up the steep drive to Cap's grandmother's and rattled to a stop beside the big house. Daddy climbed out. Jeannie couldn't seem to move.

"Get out, silly," Pearl said. "We have to meet our new friend."

Jeannie slid down from the truck seat, keeping the pie

plate balanced. Up on the veranda, the screen door was pushed open by a cane. Old Mrs. Parker came through. Her black dress reached her ankles but, from the ground, Jeannie could see the metal braces clamped to her heavy boots; she'd never thought about them before when she'd seen Mrs. Parker in church.

A woman about Mama's age joined Mrs. Parker. Papa took off his hat as he climbed the steps. "Hello, Mrs. Parker," he said, "and Mrs. Parker." He shook hands with them both. Jeannie couldn't hear the rest. Daddy was pointing to Pearl, who smiled at them, and Ella, who peeked out from behind Pearl's back.

Jeannie, feeling downright uncomfortable now, followed Pearl up the steps.

"My wife," Daddy was telling them, "says welcome and sent this baking. And this here's Jeannie. She thought it'd be nice to –" Jeannie shot him a warning look. "*Ahh . . . ,*" he continued, "to come along and say hello to your young fella, the one she's in school with."

Jeannie's face got red. *Why did Daddy have to say that?*

"That's really nice of you, Jeannie, but he's not home, I'm afraid," Cap's mother said. "Off exploring, as always. He loves it here, for sure. Just like his father."

Daddy said, "Alf and I were boys together, of course. And in the army. I've wanted to tell you how sorry I am for your loss."

"Why don't we sit down?" old Mrs. Parker offered. "Here, on the veranda, if you don't mind, John. The house is in a bit of a tizzy right now." She turned to her daughter-in-law. "Dear, why don't you cut this lovely blueberry pie and bring out some glasses of water?"

"I'll carry it in for you," Jeannie offered.

"No!" exclaimed Cap's mother. "I mean, don't trouble yourself, dear. I'll be right out. I'll get Moira, too."

Jeannie had to hand the dish over. She soon heard a voice call "Auntie?" and her heart thudded. She was pretty sure it wasn't the voice of a four-year-old.

Young Moira bounced out the door ahead of her mother and stopped a foot from Pearl and Ella. All three were the same height, Jeannie saw.

"Hello," the child said. "What's your names?"

"I'm Pearl and this is Ella and you're Moira. This is my doll, Sookie, and this is Ella's doll, Sally, and this one's for you. You can name it anything you want. It was my sister's, but she's letting you have it 'cause you don't have a daddy 'cause your poor daddy died from the war."

Jeannie bit her lip hard, but Moira accepted Pearl's speech and the doll. "She's pretty," she said. "Want to play? Gran lets me play in the barn," she told them as they started down the steps, "so I won't make noise in the house."

Daddy called, "Mind you don't go far, girls. We can't stay long."

Old Mrs. Parker sat with her veiny hands resting in her lap. Cap's mother busied herself handing out slices of pie and glasses of water.

This is not working, Jeannie thought, while the grownups talked about the war and the valley and the weather. *I can't leave without even meeting her. She's right on the other side of this wall, I bet!*

Too soon, Daddy put his empty dish down and picked up his hat from his knee. *Too soon!* It wasn't quite an accident that Jeannie's spoon flicked her last bite of blueberry pie onto her own dress at that instant. She jumped up.

"Oh, no!" she exclaimed. "Blueberry stain! It'll be okay if I rinse it out right away. Excuse me." She rushed through the screen door before anyone could stop her and hurried to the sink pump.

She could hear Cap's mother calling to her, and old Mrs. Parker saying, "Let her be, dear."

Jeannie furiously cranked the pump so she wouldn't hear anyone call her back. She lifted the hem of her dress and sloshed cool water on it. There'd be a stain for sure. She hoped it would be worth it.

"There. That'll have to do," Jeannie mumbled. She stood still and listened.

"Auntie?" a voice called softly from a side room. "Have they gone yet?"

Jeannie took a deep breath and crossed the linoleum floor as quietly as she could. Her heart hammered in her chest. *This is the right thing to do.*

The door was ajar. Jeannie pushed and it glided silently open. The foot of a bed came into view, a sewing basket resting on the chenille bedspread. The girl was sitting in a wheelchair, leaning forward to peer around the heavy drape at the window. Her hair was blonde, longer and lighter than Verity Campbell's, and held back with an emerald ribbon exactly like the one Pearl had given Jeannie. The girl pushed her hair back from her face. She was as pretty as a young movie star. A blanket lay at her feet. Below her short cotton nightgown one leg was slender, the other one pitifully shriveled.

"Oh," Jeannie said, as much for the girl's beauty as for her poor leg.

The girl swung her head around. Surprise changed to a scowl. "Who let you come in here?" she challenged. "Auntie!" she called.

Jeannie almost ran. "I'm Jeannie Shaw," she said quickly. "I'm pleased to meet you. I'm in school with Cap."

"Auntie!" the girl cried again, but no one came. She reached for the blanket.

"I'll get it," Jeannie offered and strode into the room.

"No!" the girl ordered, swinging her wheelchair to hide her legs. She struggled to reach the blanket, but Jeannie got to it first and handed it over without coming around the chair.

"Why are you here?" the girl demanded.

"I go to school with Cap," Jeannie repeated lamely.

"So what?"

"So . . . I was hoping we could get to know each other."

"Did Cap set this up – the little toad?"

"No! Cap wouldn't do that. My sister, Pearl, and my cousin Ella? They're both four. We brought them to meet Moira. I heard you when I came in." Jeannie held up the hem of her dress. "I just made this dress last week. I got blueberry juice on it and had to rinse it off. Blueberry leaves an awful stain. . . ."

The girl cast her glance over the dress.

"I don't much like making clothes," Jeannie said, "but it saves money. Do you sew?" she asked, pointing to the basket on the bed.

The girl ignored the question.

"I think I made it too short," Jeannie added. "It shows my skinny legs. Oh!" She clapped a hand over her mouth.

The hateful scowl was back. The girl spun her wheel-chair away. "Get out," she ordered.

"Please," Jeannie tried. "I'm sorry. I say stupid things, but I don't mean to. I just want to be friendly. There aren't many girls in our school. The ones there are, they're as mean as snakes."

The girl turned one wheel to look at Jeannie more directly.

"What's your name?" Jeannie asked, pretending not to know.

"Essie."

"I'm so glad to meet you, Essie." Jeannie cast around for something to talk about. A stack of books by the bed. "I love to read," she said. "Do you read a lot?"

"What do you think? It's not like I can do much else."

Jeannie was afraid to speak for fear of saying the wrong thing, and afraid not to for fear of losing this chance. *What if it were me in that wheelchair?* she wondered. *What if my father had died? If I had to move away, without Mama? I wish I had time to think! To sort out the right way to act.*

But there was no time. She reached for the top book. "I loved *Robinson Crusoe*," she commented.

Essie eyed Jeannie. "It's okay," she said.

Jeannie picked up another book. "What's this one, *The Hobbit*?"

Essie eased her wheelchair around. She held her hand out for the book and hugged it to her. "My mother ordered it special from England. This is the best book in the whole world. I don't know what I'll do when I finish it."

"Like saying good-bye to a friend," Jeannie agreed.

Essie smiled for the first time.

"I wish we had a library here," Jeannie went on, breathing easier and feeling on safer ground. "The nearest one's in Inverness. My dad drives me there once a month, but they only let you take out three books."

"My mother sends me a book a week," Essie told her. "Trying to make up for dumping me in this stupid backwoods."

"This isn't a backwoods," Jeannie insisted. "Well, not really. Mrs. Campbell says she might even start a soda fountain at the store next summer, there's so many people out on drives in the nice weather. Anyway, it's awful pretty here in the fall. Wait 'til you see the valley all orange and gold in another month! And the snowfall on the hills, after that. Sure it's quiet. And it doesn't have a library, but –"

"Or theaters, or stores," Essie cut in, "or sidewalks."

"My mother," Jeannie proclaimed, hands on hips, "says there may be places in the world as nice as the Margaree, but there's nowhere nicer."

Essie actually smirked. "And this is definitely nowhere." She stared out the window. "They think the country air will be a miracle cure for me, I suppose."

"Well, at least we haven't had one case of polio here!"

Essie glared at her. Then she laughed, a real laugh. Jeannie couldn't believe it.

"You said the *P* word," Essie mocked. "No one, except maybe the doctors, dares say the *P* word. Everyone walks on eggshells to keep from saying it. They pretend I'm still normal."

"They don't want to upset you, is all," Jeannie said.

"Please! Being around a cripple scares their blood cold."

"It doesn't scare me . . . really." She watched Essie for a moment. "Does it scare you?"

When Essie's cheeks went pale, Jeannie was sure she'd said the wrong thing yet again.

Essie barely breathed her answer. "All the time."

"It must be awful for you," Jeannie said. "I guess I'd be mad as heck."

"Don't be so prissy," Essie bullied. "It's hell, not heck."

Jeannie smiled. "Hell," she said. "Hell, hell, hell."

Essie laughed and joined in. "Hell, hell, HELL!" they yelled.

They heard the screen door open. "Essie, dear," called her aunt, "is everything all right?"

"Yes. Leave us alone," Essie called back. She saw the look on Jeannie's face and added "please."

Jeannie couldn't wait to tell Cap how wrong he'd been. *This is my friend, Essie,* she thought. It sounded even more wonderful than "Cecilia." Her wish had come perfectly true. And here she was, having a real friendly visit with the new girl.

"What are you sewing?" Jeannie asked as she lifted a length of clean flour bag from the basket.

"I sewed my own costumes for some plays I was in, you know." Essie shrugged. "Now the old granny's got me stitching our underwear from those bags. Can you believe it? Says I should be thankful my arms work and I should 'offer each stitch to the Lord.'" Essie rolled her eyes. "What an old witch."

Jeannie ignored the lack of respect. "You could still use that, couldn't you?" she asked, pointing to the Singer treadle sewing machine under a dustcover and pushed against the wall. "It only takes one foot to work the pedal . . . if you don't mind my saying."

Essie eyed the closed sewing machine with a spark of interest. "I haven't made anything in two years. I don't know. . . ."

"I could help," Jeannie offered. She pulled the sewing basket to the edge of the bed so they could look through it together. "What supplies do you have? We have tons. I'll bring my patterns over next time. We're about the same size, I bet." She smiled at Essie. "You know, you have such pretty hair. Verity Campbell is going to turn pure green with envy when she sees it."

Essie cringed. "NO! Don't be telling anyone I'm here. Not anyone!"

"I won't, I promise! Not if you don't want me to. See? Cross my heart and hope to die. But –"

Essie shook her head in violent refusal to listen. The golden hair swung like wings. She seized and twisted at the arms of her wheelchair, her mood all thunder and lightning again. "I . . . was supposed to be . . . an actress!" she ground out through her tight-set jaw. "Not a movie star, a stage actress! All my life, that's what I longed for. I've been in five plays, you know. Five! Then this happened. Now I'm ugly."

"No, you're not!" Jeannie protested. "You're still so beautiful."

"Look at me," Essie cried. "Look!" She flung the blanket away. Her perfect leg next to the other one – curved in, twig thin.

Jeannie reached a hand to the stricken girl's shoulder.

"Don't," Essie sobbed. "Don't you dare pity me!" She swung her arm wide to knock Jeannie's hand away, but knocked over the sewing basket instead. Thread spools and scissors and rickrack spread across the bed. "I'm a cripple. I am *not* beautiful!" She grabbed up the sewing shears. "And the faster I get used to it, the better off I'll be, right?"

Jeannie staggered back as the scissors swung. "Daddy," she whimpered, unable to look away.

Essie reached around with her other hand and grabbed a fistful of her own perfectly beautiful, movie-star hair. *Chop!* went the scissors, and a chunk of hair fell to the floor like spilled sunshine. Essie was groaning more than sobbing, the sounds churning up from deep inside. *Chop!* Golden locks tumbled through golden evening light from the window.

"Daddy!" Jeannie shrieked. "Mrs. Parker!"

Essie switched hands and reached far up her hair. *Chop! Chop!* She flung hanks of hair at Jeannie, who covered her face and cowered against the wall.

Feet came running. "Come away, Jeannie," Daddy ordered and pulled her toward the door. Cap's mother wrung her hands, but Essie had already stopped hacking at her poor hair and was sobbing into the crook of her elbow.

Old Mrs. Parker arrived, her heavy canes thunking. "I'll have those scissors," she said calmly. "You've done enough hairdressing for today, I think."

Daddy guided Jeannie through the kitchen and down the steps. "Stay here," he said at the truck. "I have to get Pearl and Ella from the barn." He hurried away.

Jeannie's shaking hands covered her ears to block out the keening cries from the house. Old Mrs. Parker came out onto the veranda. Daddy returned with the little girls, Ella quiet and Pearl complaining loudly that they weren't done playing yet. Moira followed behind, clutching the doll she'd been given.

"Get in the truck, Pearl," Daddy rumbled. "Right now, or I swear. . . ." Jeannie climbed in after the girls and stared straight ahead.

Daddy lifted his hat as he came around the hood of the truck. "Good-bye, Mrs. Parker," he said. "We're awful sorry for causing you more grief."

Mrs. Parker nodded and offered a weary smile.

"Who's crying?" Pearl wanted to know.

Daddy got in and started the noisy engine, drowning out all other sounds.

They rattled down the rutted driveway. At the bottom, Daddy almost hit Cap Parker, carrying a rifle over one shoulder and a canvas knapsack on the other. Cap jumped clear.

Jeannie saw his surprise change to recognition as Daddy hit the brake and called out, "Sorry, son."

Cap waved good-naturedly. He glanced up the hill toward his grandmother's house, then back to Jeannie. A frown took over from the smile.

Daddy started off again and they drove home in a cloud of dust. Jeannie felt a tickle on her hand. She looked down and plucked sun-gold strands of Essie's hair from a fold of her dress. She held them out the window, and finally let them go.

When they got home, Pearl was happy to be sent to play with Ella. Daddy stood in the doorway and watched until the little ones got to Auntie Libby's house. Then he turned, leaned his shoulder on the doorjamb, and crossed his arms. Mama's arms were crossed, too, above her belly.

Jeannie told them everything – that Cap had warned her not to go, what had happened in Essie's room.

At the end of it all Daddy said, "I'm disappointed in you, Jeannie. You stuck your nose in where it wasn't wanted. You did harm to that family. Sure, you meant well," he cut in when she tried to defend herself, "but when are you going to stop assuming you know best?"

"That's not the way it was at all!" Jeannie protested. "I needed to meet her."

"I don't think she needed to meet you, Jeannie," Mama said.

Jeannie slumped in the chair. "I never meant for this to happen. I'm sorry."

"We're not the ones who need to hear it," Daddy told her.

"I'll write an apology to Essie and give it to Cap at school."

"Write another one to the family," Mama added.

Up in her room, Jeannie wrote the note to Cap's mother and grandmother. Then she wrote for ages, scratching out, throwing out half-started versions of a longer apology to Essie. It was almost midnight when she blew out the lamp, her eyes gritty with sleepy sadness.

In the morning, Jeannie puttered around, taking ages to get ready for school.

"That's enough," Mama ordered. "You've never been late and you're not going to start today. Your troubles aren't going to disappear while you dillydally at home. Face your demons, as they say."

At least she didn't meet anyone on the road. She got to school just as Mousie came out to ring the bell. It clanged through her aching head as she took her place in the senior line. Cap, ahead of her, didn't turn around.

He didn't look over when they stood to sing the anthem, or when they went out at recess, then at lunch. Jeannie tried to move her feet forward to approach him, but her mind kept her rooted in place. Twice she opened her mouth to speak while they were settling in their seats after lunch, but she couldn't get the words out.

I'm such a coward, she scolded herself.

She pulled the letters out of her geography book and stared at the cream parchment envelope on top, with "Essie" written in the middle. It felt cool and rich, her birthday stationery from Auntie Libby last year. A whole year had passed and she'd never had anyone to write to before now.

She forced herself to slide the letters across her side of the desk. She waited for Cap to notice. *Doesn't he see?* She wiggled them. No response. Jeannie swallowed hard and gave up, slipping the envelopes back into her textbook.

When the bell rang, she shuffled her books until everyone else had left. When Mousie went out behind them all to make sure they behaved like ladies and gentlemen, Jeannie rose to go home.

Cap was standing in the doorway. He shook his head when Jeannie tried to speak. He held out his hand. "The letters," he said.

Jeannie put them in his hand.

"I have a message, too," he said. Hope flared in her heart. "From my gran," he went on. "She says not to feel too bad. She says to tell you 'crisis is catalyst.' I promised Gran I'd tell you exactly that." And he left.

Jeannie went to the big dictionary in the bookshelf and carried it to her desk. "Crisis," she read aloud, "the turning point, for better or worse." There was more, but none of it was very positive. She finally found the second word when she figured out it had a letter *y* in it. "Catalyst: 1) an agent that induces or speeds up a change without itself undergoing change. 2) one who unintentionally causes a change."

She thumped the dictionary shut. The definitions fit together, she accepted, all but where it said "without itself undergoing change."

"Crisis is catalyst," she repeated as she walked home. "Sounds like something Mama would say." *I'm a crisis.*

12

*J*eannie lay in bed the next morning and thought over all that had happened. Cap's grandmother was right. She wasn't just a crisis; she was a catalyst. She had to believe that.

Mama didn't need to hurry her after breakfast. Jeannie was at school early, sure that Cap would bring word from Essie.

When he arrived at the last minute, he wouldn't look her way. Jeannie had to wait until recess to pull him aside. "You have to tell me what she said. Did Essie send me a note back?"

Cap shrugged. "Far as I know, she didn't even open yours."

Jeannie looked at the ground. *So. This is my punishment.*

"Look," Cap said, sounding a tiny bit sorry for her. "I tried to give it to her, honest, but she wouldn't take it. I left it on her bed. It was still there when I got up this morning. Hey, at least she didn't cut it up with the scissors, right?"

Jeannie nodded. She wandered through the afternoon lessons, getting easy math problems wrong, misspelling words like "power" and "watt."

This is the worst thing that's ever happened to me, she thought. And then she went home.

Her parents didn't mention Essie Phalen again and neither did she. Daddy took the truck to Phillips' Garage to get a radiator leak checked. Mama was catching up with the laundry left undone while Pearl was sick.

Pearl's wasp stings had almost disappeared and she was herself again, which meant she had disappeared, too. Mama declared, "The day's almost over and I'm still doing laundry. I'll have to put it on the line overnight. I'm too busy to chase after that child one more time! When you find her, Jeannie, come right back and help with the rinsing."

Jeannie called Pearl from the steps. No answer. She searched in the barn, at the swing, in the lean-to around back where Pearl and Ella played house.

"Lady, where's Pearl?" she asked when she had circled back to the steps. Lady stood up, already panting from the heat.

"Poor old girl," Jeannie said, "never mind. I'll keep looking."

But Lady maneuvered down the steps and across the yard. She sniffed under the swing.

"Was she here?" Jeannie asked as Lady started along the path. "Did she come this way? Good girl!" But Pearl was not at the stream, either. "Oh, Lady," Jeannie said, "you don't really know where she is, do you? Go on back to the step, you silly old dog."

Lady's head bobbed up and down in the effort to catch her breath. But she kept going beside the stream, the farthest she'd been in a year or more.

"Pearl?" Jeannie called, getting worried now.

Lady fumbled her way over tree roots in the path. She woofed and hurried a little.

Before she saw Pearl, Jeannie heard her childish voice singing. Beyond the next bend, Jeannie stepped over Lady, who, her mission accomplished, had promptly laid herself down in the pine needles to recover.

Pearl was belly down over a fallen log that had lodged, suspended, between two crisscrossed trees. She was swinging her feet, drawing with a twig in the debris of the forest floor, and singing "Old MacDonald Had a Farm."

"Pearl, why didn't you answer me? You must've heard me yelling!"

"*Ee-i-ee-i-ohhh*," Pearl ended, off tune. "I wasn't finished my song yet, that's why."

Jeannie clenched her hands into fists. "Come home right now," she ordered. "You know you're not supposed to be at the stream by yourself."

"I'm not. The stream's way over there." Pearl pointed to the water, two steps away. "Lady and I were playing hide-and-seek." She flopped onto the dog and hugged her. "Good doggie! Now it's your turn, Lady." She ran back along the path, counting, "One, two, three. . . ."

"*Ooh*, she drives me crazy," Jeannie muttered, following after. "C'mon, Lady. Home!"

Back at the house, Pearl was sent to her room for wandering off again. Lady finally came scuffling up the steps, her tongue hanging out the side of her mouth between her few remaining teeth. And Jeannie began to help with the washing.

No more than ten minutes later, Barncat, dressed in doll clothes, came tearing through the kitchen while Mama was scrubbing Daddy's shirt collars at the sink. Jeannie caught Barncat easily, when he tripped over the dragging hem of a frilly smock. She freed him and let him out the screen door just as Pearl skipped into the kitchen.

"Why'd you do that, Jeannie? Barncat wanted to play school with me, y'know!"

"Because I'm a bad sister," Jeannie said and returned to rinsing clothes in the big metal tub.

"Yes, you are," Pearl agreed. "Mama, read to me, please, please."

"Sorry, Pearl. I don't have time."

"But you read to me yesterday."

"You were sick then."

"I'm still sick. *Ooh,* I feel all whooshy!"

"Go to bed," Jeannie suggested. "The stairs are that way."

"You're mean! You're my mean, ugly stepsister."

Jeannie guided a sheet through the wringer. "And just yesterday you told me I was pretty."

"Well, everyone was nice to me yesterday. No one cares about poor Pearlie today!"

" 'For I am poor and needy, and my heart is wounded within me,' " Mama recited. "It's a wash day, child," she reminded Pearl, through the steam of the laundry tub. "You're welcome to help. I'll show you how to scrub Daddy's work socks. How about that?"

Pearl disappeared out the door.

"Thought that might work," Mama said.

Pearl was soon back looking for something to eat. Mama dried her hands and spread molasses on biscuits. Back again, wanting a drink. Mama dried her hands to pump a glass of water. A minute later Pearl returned.

"Jeannie's birthday is coming," she announced, heading for the pantry. "I'm gonna bake her a cake, even if she is mean."

Sometimes Mama let her play with the utensils, pretending to bake. But not on a wash day. Jeannie looked at Mama, who shut her eyes for a moment.

Pearl called from the pantry, "Mama, can you get the big bowl down? I need the measuring cups, Mama. And I need the wooden spoon and –"

Mama dropped the yellow bar of Sunlight soap into the tub. Clouds of suds puffed into the air. "Pearl Shaw," she yelled, "you'll get the wooden spoon, all right! Now get out of there before I take it to your bottom!"

It's about time, Jeannie thought.

Pearl appeared in the pantry doorway, her mouth stretched down at the corners. She crossed her arms. As ferociously as her chunky little legs would carry her, she stomped across the kitchen, out the door, and plopped down on the top step, loudly complaining to Lady.

Mama plopped down, too, in a chair and wiped her face with her apron. "That child is driving me foolish," she muttered.

"Mama?" Jeannie began. "I was going to pick one more batch of blueberries for the store. I could take Pearl with me. If she'd leave the wasp nests alone."

Mama looked up. "That would be a blessing," she said.

As soon as she was told, Pearl declared that Jeannie wasn't an ugly stepsister anymore. Then she remembered. "But Ella's coming over."

"Oh. That's right," Mama said. "Auntie Libby is bringing me Ella's baby clothes." She sighed. "Never mind, Jeannie. They wanted to play together."

"No," Jeannie said, trying to sound as if she meant it. "I'll take them both."

"Hooray!" Pearl shouted and ran outside.

"They're a lot to handle, dear," Mama warned. "You don't have to take them." But she didn't sound as if she really meant it, either.

Jeannie shrugged. "It's all right. They'd only drive you crazy. Now you can talk your heads off about Tina's perfect wedding. Anyway, they're like you and Auntie Libby – best friends."

"Jeannie, you'll have a best friend, too, someday. I promise."

"What are you going to do, order me one from the Eaton's catalogue?"

Mama smiled. "I'm going to sit right down and do that very thing; see if I don't."

A shout told them Pearl had caught sight of Ella coming across the field. Jeannie dried her hands and stepped out to the veranda. After a minute, Mama came out, too. She handed Jeannie a paper bag. "Daddy and I are having boiled salt mackerel for supper. Thought you'd prefer a picnic."

Pearl and Ella bounced around Auntie Libby in the high grass, but all you could see of the little ones was

Pearl's halo of honey-colored hair and Ella's, smooth and brown.

"Those two must've eaten chair springs for breakfast," Mama said.

"Was I as much of a handful as Pearl?" Jeannie asked.

"No, my dear. You were always the perfect child, just as Pearl will have been when I tell her about herself in years to come."

"You forgive everything she does."

"She's just a child," Mama said. "Besides, 'to err is human; to forgive, divine.' You always forgive family."

While the grown-up sisters poured tea and sorted baby clothes, Jeannie and the little girls trooped up the hill. The sun beat down on the berry meadow. *At least it's better than doing laundry,* Jeannie told herself.

"Look, Ella," Pearl called, "millions of blueberries!" Ella ran to join her.

"Pearl," Ella cried later, "there's lots and lots over here!" And Pearl ran to her cousin. Every time they collected a few in their tin cups, they dumped them in the big pail. Jeannie cleaned out leaves and stems when they did.

At suppertime, they picnicked beside the shallow stream in the shade of the forest. They ate biscuits with ham and cheese, apples, and gingersnaps. They pulled off their shoes and socks to wade, and scooped water to drink. All three came out dripping wet and cooler.

As they sat under the trees, Jeannie laid small twigs in a row on a flat stone, then slotted more twigs under and over those to weave a square.

"What's that?" Ella wanted to know.

"The roof of a fairy house," Jeannie told her. "Here. I'll show you what I used to do."

She brushed aside layers of pine needles between the tree roots. In the soft earth beneath, she stuck twigs in line to form walls of a tiny house, with space for a doorway. She laid the woven square on top, then small mats of moss to cover the roof.

"Now for the door."

The little girls leaned right in to see. Jeannie poked three holes along one side of a birch leaf. With a skinny twig slotted through the holes, she positioned it in the doorway.

"There you are," she said. "Done! A fairy house."

Pearl pushed the leaf on its hinge. "It really opens!"

Jeannie taught them how to weave the twig squares. The little girls cleared paths from one tree root to the next for roads and created a whole village. They planted fairy vegetable gardens, with tiny round tamarack cones as cabbages, scraps of moss as lettuce. They fashioned a fairy fishing boat out of bark and laid it beside a twig dock in a quiet corner of the stream.

"Well," Jeannie said, imitating Mrs. Campbell, "this will never put jam on the table. Come on, girls."

"No," Pearl said. "We want to play. It's no fun picking anymore."

"It's not supposed to be fun. You have to help," Jeannie said. "Fine. See if I care." She started back to the berry meadow, calling over her shoulder, "But don't let the Bochdan catch you."

Ella's head whipped around. "What?"

Jeannie stopped and looked back. "Don't you know? This is the Bochdan's brook. See the big rock in the middle? Long ago, that's where a wicked thief got buried, under that rock. Now he comes to haunt lazy children who sit by his brook and don't help."

Ella backed away from the water's edge. Pearl kept right on weaving a fairy roof. "Don't listen, Ella," she said. "She's just being stupid. The Bochdan lives way over behind Campbell's Store. Everybody knows that. He caught Mrs. Campbell once, but he sent her back real fast 'cause she never stops yakking."

Jeannie's jaw dropped. "Who told you that?"

"Daddy did. And he doesn't make up lies like you do, Jeannie Shaw."

"Pearl," Jeannie ordered, "you come help right now, or I'll be telling Daddy about you!"

Pearl sighed and got to her feet. She took Ella's hand. "Don't worry, Ella," she said. "Meanie Jeannie's the only scary monster around here." And they tromped back out to the meadow.

They ate more berries than they put in their tin cups. They chased each other and trampled berry bushes when they hid in them, until Jeannie gave up. "You two are pests!" she complained. "Go on back to the stream and be good. Don't go across it, you hear?"

"Yippee!" cried Pearl. "C'mon, Ella. Bring your cup. We'll collect things for our village."

Jeannie bent to her picking. After a moment she stood again to call, as Mama used to call to her, "Mind you stay in sight, girls. Pearl?"

Halfway across the clearing, Pearl turned at the faint sound of her name and waved, as if she'd heard.

Jeannie could see the girls playing. She could dimly hear them chattering and singing.

As she plucked warm berries, she daydreamed of having a friend of her own. Someone she could visit, in a cool house, where no jam was being made. At least dreams did no harm. When she finished picking, she leaned back to rest for a moment with her arm shading her eyes. The next minute she really was dreaming.

An ant crawling on her hand woke her. Jeannie shielded her eyes in amazement at the sun lying so low in the west. She shook her head to clear it and squinted toward the stream, hidden now in deep tree shadows.

"Girls," she called wearily, "let's go." She picked up the full pail. "Pearl . . . Ella," she called around the edges of a yawn.

No reply.

"Pearl Shaw, answer me this instant!"

Nothing.

"Oh, my!" Jeannie dropped the pail, and her shoes crushed spilled dark berries as she ran to the stream.

But no Pearl. No Ella.

She scrambled through bushes, calling all the while, then made herself be still and listen. Everything had hushed but the bees. *How could such little girls get so far away so fast?*

"PEARL!" Jeannie screamed, hurting her throat. "I'm going to get Mama. I'm going to get her right now, so you better come out if this is one of your games. Even Mama won't forgive you this time, scaring us so!"

She splashed right into the water, shoes and all. She searched upstream and down, until she was hoarse with shouting. Each time she yelled, she was sure the girls would answer at last. After a long while, she was sure they wouldn't.

"No," Jeannie whispered. "Oh, no."

She yanked the green ribbon from her hair, the one Pearl had given her, and held it up like a banner. "If you come out now," she yelled, "you can have my new ribbon, I promise. Please?" She held her breath until it came out as a sob.

"I'm going to get Mama!" she called again. Now it was a promise, not a threat. She tied the ribbon on a branch. It was all she could think of to do, to leave as a sign to the girls. Then she ran like wildfire was chasing her. Branches snagged her hair and whipped at her bare arms. Tree roots on the forest path seemed to rise up with a will to trip her. Her eyes were so full of tears, the only way she made it back was that her feet knew the way.

When she came in sight of the house, Mama was pinning a baby quilt on the clothesline and pushing the line back up with the wooden clothes prop. Mama looked up, smiled, thinking it was a race with the little ones, perhaps. She shaded her eyes with her hand. When she saw Jeannie better, her hand dropped and the color drained from her face.

"What's happened?" Mama cried. "Where are the girls?"

Jeannie staggered to a stop in front of her. She bent double, gripping the clothes prop, trying to get her breath. When she could speak at all, she gasped out, "They were there, by the stream. I could hear them. They were there, Mama! Singing, playing. I fell asleep. I didn't mean to. Oh, Mama, what have I done? I should never have —"

"How long ago?" Mama demanded.

Auntie Libby came out the door with another quilt over her arm. Jeannie watched her aunt wave to her. "I didn't mean to. . . ."

Mama gripped her daughter's shoulders. "How long, child?"

"I don't know. I searched forever. An hour, maybe? I don't know!"

"Get your father." Mama shook her once. "Jeannie, listen to me! Down at the garage. Run and get your father! Tell him, likely we'll have found them by the time he gets here. Tell him that!"

Jeannie ran again, with barely breath or strength, down the endless dusty road. She pressed her fist into the stitch in her side. Daddy was there, talking to Mr. Phillips, who had his head under the hood of the truck. She could see Daddy's smile disappear, as Mama's had, as she got closer.

Again she tried to speak. All that came out was "Lost!"

Daddy said one word – "Pearl." Flat, like he'd already known. He left Jeannie there and ran.

Jeannie wobbled. She could feel the muscles in her legs twitching, ticking over like the truck engine as it settled after a drive. Mr. Phillips guided her to the old car seat he kept by the door. She heard him go in and lift the phone receiver. He got Mrs. MacDonald to connect him with the RCMP detachment in Inverness.

When he came back, he led Jeannie to his truck, saying, "Constable Hennessy's on his way. I'll drive you back, then round up some folks. Thelma MacDonald was listening, like usual. She'll spread the word, too. Don't you worry. Your parents probably found those kiddies already, but . . . just in case." He kept talking the whole way.

Before the truck rattled to a stop, Jeannie yanked the door open, slid down off the seat, and ran to the house. It was empty. She shook her head to Mr. Phillips, who raced his truck backwards down their driveway in a storm of dust.

Jeannie headed up the hill, hoping she'd see two little girls being scolded for causing such a commotion. Her parents and aunt were just emerging from the forest shadows.

"Please," Jeannie muttered. "You can have all my ribbons, Pearl. Just please. . . ."

But no Pearl. No Ella.

Daddy cupped his hands around his mouth and bellowed, "PEARL! ELLA!" If little voices answered, no one heard.

Jeannie couldn't look at her parents. "I'm so sorry," she choked out.

Her mother put an arm around her, but managed no comforting words. Any other time, at a scraped knee or a cold, Mama always said, "I pity you, I pity you, I pity you," her benediction.

Auntie Libby wrung her hands and made small noises. She didn't once look at Jeannie. Daddy stood to the side, with his hands shoved into the back pockets of his overalls. He stared at the woods, trying to see through them.

A handful of neighbors arrived, hurrying Mr. Phillips ahead of them up the hill. Two had brought their hunting dogs.

Daddy squinted to look around the crowd gathering in the clearing. "We appreciate this, folks," he began. "Fan out from here to the power line cutting and work down 'til you hit the wood road. Shout if you find any sign of them. We haven't got long before dark. Let's hope. . . ." He didn't finish. "Jeannie," he said, "you go back home. When Constable Hennessy arrives, send him up, then stay at the house in case the girls show up there."

"But, Daddy, I can't just –"

He was already striding across the clearing. Mama said, "Do what he says, honey."

Then everyone, even Mama, stepped into the gloom of the forest and was gone, leaving Jeannie alone in the meadow. She turned this way and that, as if lost herself. She hid her face in her hands.

When she lifted her head again, she took great heaving breaths. The sun hid below the hills now, but heat still lay in the clearing, cooking the spilled pails of ripe blueberries, trampled and forgotten. The air was heavy with their sweetness. In years to come, Jeannie would still help make jam. The pot would just start to heat up, and it would all come back to her – the smell of that afternoon.

She stumbled down the hill and waited at the house. Constable Hennessy arrived, then Mr. Campbell from the store. They headed up to join the others. The rest of the time, Jeannie stood alone in the yard where she could see as far as possible. There was a scuffling sound and she turned to find Lady waddling stiffly across the dirt yard. They stood together while calling voices echoed off the hills, as if even the ghosts of the Margaree had risen to join the search.

As dusk became darkness, the searchers straggled back, hardly speaking. Mama cradled two little pairs of shoes and socks in the crook of her arm. She looked stricken as she told Jeannie, "They waded in the stream, I guess. The dogs couldn't catch any scent of them from there."

The constable asked for everyone's attention. "Go home now," he called, and Jeannie's gut burned with fear. "Go home, those that need to," he said, "and get ready for a night in the woods. Flashlights, lanterns, jackets. We'll leave word at the post office switchboard if there's any news. Meet back here and you'll be assigned a search area. Bring others. There's lots of woods out there. . . ."

Mama put her arm around Auntie Libby's shoulders. Jeannie's heart felt like it was on fire and she had to look away. In the headlamps of a departing truck, she caught sight of Daddy talking with Constable Hennessy and she worked her way through the crowd to be closer to him.

"John?" Mama had come up behind Jeannie. Daddy turned. He carried his flashlight and his compass.

"I have to go," he told her.

"I know. Oh, John, I can't bear this!"

Neither could Jeannie. What had she done to her family? They would never forgive her for this. *Let me be the one who's lost,* she thought.

"Try not to worry," Daddy said, and kissed his wife's forehead. "You have to think of the baby. Jeannie, help your mother all you can." He kissed Jeannie, too, and he was gone. Soon everyone was gone.

She watched the spots of the flashlights until she couldn't tell them from the fireflies. *Help Mama? How can I even face her?* Jeannie's heart would burst from the pain in it, she felt sure. A sob came out.

"There, there," Mama said, distracted, still watching the darkness.

"I can't help it. How can you even stand me? It's all my fault!"

"What are you talking about, child?"

"I shouldn't have lost them."

"Listen to me." Mama stepped back and took Jeannie's chin in her hand. "Look at me. There is nothing that could make us stop loving you, you hear? Nothing! This is a terrible trouble, but we'll have to hope for the best and get through it. Together. That's what this family does, understand?" She held on to Jeannie's chin and waited. Jeannie finally nodded, then leaned against her mother's rounded apron front and sobbed out the hot pain.

They stayed on the veranda until the cuckoo clock cried midnight. Mama said, "We'll leave a lamp burning in the porch tonight, dear." She went in.

Jeannie whispered, "Pearl," and went in, too.

CHAPTER

13

Neither of them slept. They sat in hot chairs and listened to the house creak.

Near dawn, Jeannie helped Mama bake double batches of biscuits. Friends and neighbors, family and strangers, kept showing up to search for the little girls. Lady stood up when the first dogs arrived. She eased herself down the steps and sniffed with matronly dignity, while the younger dogs barked and raced around. Then she stood by Mama to make it clear just who belonged here and who were the visitors.

Dr. Andrews arrived, then Father MacNeil with Rev. and Mrs. Hope, then ministers and priests from all the other churches. Tina's fiancé, Edwin, arrived, still wearing his fishing gear. A dozen other fishermen, too. From Judique to Cheticamp, they'd left their boats in harbor and come inland on the search for the two little girls.

Edwin stepped forward. "Morning, Mrs. Shaw. Any word?" Mama shook her head.

She and Jeannie had washed the good china and laid it out on the veranda table. They'd made a huge pot of coffee, but nobody stopped to drink any. Mama sent Jeannie to wrap a couple of biscuits each in twists of waxed paper, to hand to people as they headed out on the search.

Lady followed the dogs to the edge of the yard. She sniffed the ground halfheartedly, as if she wondered what all the fuss was about. Mama was holding the doll she'd brought from Pearl's bed to give the dogs the scent. Lady nudged it where it dangled from Mama's hand.

"If anyone sees John," Mama called to the searchers, "send word!"

At seven o'clock, Mr. and Mrs. Campbell arrived. "The store won't fall apart in one day," Mrs. Campbell pronounced. "We had to be here."

The senior class came up the drive next, Mr. Moss and Verity Campbell in front, then Sarah and Melanie, John Angus and Dougald. No sign of Cap Parker.

"Miss MacQueen," the principal stated, "sends her deepest sympathies and hopes, Mrs. Shaw. I am breaking several school board rules, but we had to be here," he added, echoing Mrs. Campbell.

Verity, Sarah, and Melanie rushed over to Jeannie. "Oh, Jeannie!" Sarah said and commenced to weep. Even Melanie dabbed her eyes and looked pale.

Verity's voice quavered, too, but she gave her speech. "Jeannie, we're so sorry. You can't imagine how terrible we feel. We barely slept and I couldn't eat breakfast! But they'll be found, we just know it." Sarah and Melanie bobbed their heads.

Yesterday Jeannie would have been thrilled to have these girls standing in her yard, being nice to her. Today all she could think was that her sister and her cousin had been lost in the woods all night. Nothing else mattered. She barely nodded at the girls. Mr. Moss marched them up the hill, still in double file.

Jeannie and her mother were cleaning up, dumping out the coffee, when Cap Parker and his three older brothers strode up the driveway, carrying hunting rifles. "Sorry we're late," the tallest told Mama. "No one out our way to give us a lift."

"You're the Parker boys," Mama said. They introduced themselves: Alf, Paul, Tam, and Cap. "You must have walked for two hours. Jeannie, pour a pitcher of water, please. And these boys aren't going anywhere before they have a bite to eat."

Jeannie was so weary and sad, it hardly registered that Cap Parker was at her house. The boys – men, really, except for Cap – thanked her for the biscuits and cheese and discussed how to begin their search. Jeannie sat on the top step and stared at nothing, tried to feel nothing.

"*Uh*, Jeannie?" It was Cap. "I just want to say, sorry for your troubles."

Jeannie didn't lift her head. "They're not dead, you know," she said.

Cap ran a hand through his hair. "Pardon?"

"People say it at funerals: 'Sorry for your troubles.' Pearl and Ella are not dead."

Cap walked away, then spun on his boot heels and returned. He shoved his hands into his pockets and bent close to talk to her. "Listen here, Jeannie. We're always gonna say the wrong thing to each other. I sure don't mean to, but I do. This must be awful hard for you and I'm real sorry. That's all I meant. Can we just call a truce for now?"

Jeannie forced her head up. "You're right. I'm sorry. I'm being mean again. I haven't done anything right for a while. And now it's my fault they're lost."

"Hey, don't say that. Even woodsmen can get lost in these hills." He struggled for words. "Mostly, see, it's a good place, especially with the weather so steady. The woods won't likely harm them."

"If that's so," she challenged, "why'd you bring your rifles?"

He shrugged. "'Cause. We're going into the woods. We probably won't need them. It's just common sense to carry them."

Jeannie looked beyond Cap to where the forest started. She'd never thought of it before, how the trees were so close that their dark branches brushed against the house, scraped the barn's shingles and spread out from there, filling her world, only stopping when the sea halted them. A few houses, a few villages. All the rest, forest and forest and forest. And two little girls. . . .

Cap's brother Paul called to him. Cap waved and turned back. "Jeannie, we need to know what the girls were wearing, things like that."

She checked with Mama about the clothes, then took the Parker boys up to where she'd seen the children last, to where she'd left the green ribbon tied to a bush.

"They had their tin cups with them," she remembered. "Those are missing, too."

"We'll start now," Cap said. "Look, I won't tell you not to worry. I guess I know how I'd feel if the pip-squeak was my sister." Jeannie's eyes teared up at the nickname. "See?" Cap said. "I always say the wrong thing!"

"No, you didn't at all! It just keeps feeling like there's a hole punched through me." Jeannie looked right at him and was startled. She'd never expected to see a boy with tears in his eyes. They both turned red and didn't know what to say.

"Hey, pip-squeak!" Paul called to him again. "Let's get moving."

Cap shook his head. "See what I have to put up with?" He crossed the clearing.

While the brothers disappeared into the forest, Jeannie watched the ribbon dangling from the branch. *Was it only yesterday I tied it there?*

Mama was in the kitchen when she got home. "I came back like you asked," Jeannie said. "Why couldn't I go on the search, too?"

"People will be arriving," Mama told her, "and they'll still need to be fed, but I can't stay here waiting. I may be in the family way, but Pearl is still my baby. And poor little Ella is out there, too. I can't stay here!" Mama didn't seem to have any idea how her words cut Jeannie.

"Mrs. Campbell brought these," Mama continued as she finished cutting up two plucked chickens and added them to the stewpot. She piled chopped vegetables onto the counter and built up the wood fire. "Look after this stew, Jeannie. Soon as the broth heats, add the vegetables. Don't try to move this big pot to the back; just keep adding a little water to the halfway mark and let the fire die down. I'll see to it when I get back." Mama tied a scarf around her hair.

Jeannie watched as her mother headed up to join the search. From the back, Mama looked like a girl, small and quick-moving.

Lady was lying in her usual spot, with something under her head. Jeannie sat beside her and saw that it was the doll Pearl called her Sookie. Lady rested her chin on it like a pillow.

"Where'd you find that?" Jeannie asked. "Where is she, Lady? Where's Pearl?" Lady lifted her head at the sound of the child's name. She stared out into the yard.

Jeannie went inside. It took forever for the broth to boil. As soon as it did, Jeannie carefully dropped in the carrots and onions, the celery and potatoes . . . and lots and lots of extra water. Then she ran. Out to the porch for her old shoes. Up to her room to stuff her pockets with every hair ribbon she owned, even the Barncat-ruined ones from her wastebasket. Down to Mama's sewing corner for all the lace she could find. She cut everything into short strands.

And Jeannie left, too.

"I can't stay here waiting, either," she told the empty house, then turned her back on it.

But which way? She didn't want to meet anyone too

soon, to have to explain herself; to have to turn back if she came across her mother. Everyone had started from the meadow where the girls had last been seen. Then the searchers had spread out, all up and down the hillsides and the valley floor.

"Which way should I go, Lady?" she asked.

Pearl's Sookie doll lay upside down on the second step, but Lady was nowhere in sight.

"Lady?" Jeannie called. "Here, Lady!" *Now where did she get to? And what way should I go?*

Downhill. Beside the water. Simple choices, ones that four-year-olds might have made. Jeannie headed along the brook path beyond the barn, leading down the valley.

At every turn in the path, she tied a ribbon or a piece of lace to a low branch, just where four-year-olds might see it. "There you are, Pearl," she said as she gave up the first one. "There's a present for you." It fluttered in the breeze.

She heard other searchers calling. When she crossed paths with any of them, they would look hopefully at her and she at them. But then they would shake their heads. If anyone asked who was with her, Jeannie would mumble about the "others" being just a little farther back. With a few words to say where they'd been, who else they'd seen, a pat on Jeannie's shoulder, they would move on. Each time someone approached, Jeannie stuffed the fistful of ribbons into her pocket. It seemed too silly to explain, this tying ribbons to branches. It felt like a connection, that was all she knew.

All day Jeannie clambered over boulders and fallen trees until she was far from their own property, but always near the water. She saw deer. She saw rabbits and a fox, but no children. Such a big land.

On the flat, the forest finally gave way to marshes, with thick bushes and head-high grasses. The stream meandered along the valley floor, bending back to form little oxbow lakes with hillock islands, before joining with other streams into a serious river, even in this dry season.

Jeannie pushed her way through and almost stepped off into a deep salmon pool. She saved herself by grabbing the sturdy reeds and got only one shoe wet. Beyond, in the middle of the marsh, a cow moose eyed her without twitching a muscle, except to chew grass roots. *Is this the same one Cap was talking about?* She hoped Pearl and Ella didn't happen upon this huge creature, its head as big as a chair. The little girls would be dwarfed by the dense marsh grasses and wouldn't even see the moose until they walked right into it. Or into the water, where Jeannie had almost landed. She stared now into the brown depths of the salmon pool, deep enough to swallow her up if she'd fallen in. Deep enough.

All the goodness in her valley grew dark and cold when Jeannie thought of the two little girls stumbling through it. She tried to ignore the scratches and bruises, the mosquitoes and no-see-ums that tortured her. *Pearl and Ella,* she kept thinking, *Pearl and Ella.* But when the fast-fading light threatened to leave her stranded, she hurriedly tied her last ribbons to branches and retreated up the valley.

"I have to go back, Pearl," she whispered. "I can't have Mama worrying about me, too. I'm sorry, girls." She touched strands of ribbon as she retraced her steps.

Daddy hadn't returned when Jeannie emerged from the dusk into the throng of anxious neighbors and relatives, nor had he been seen all the livelong day. Mama was back, though, waiting for each one in her family, holding Pearl's doll again. She saw Jeannie and strode forward.

"Where have you been?" Mama demanded, with more anger than Jeannie had ever heard. "And where's Lady? No one's seen her!"

Jeannie didn't even get a word in before Mama crumpled, her knees buckling under her. Now it was Auntie Libby who put an arm around her sister. Jeannie ran forward to help her mother up from the grass, but was pushed aside.

"I'll look after her! You've done enough damage!" Auntie Libby snapped. Jeannie staggered back.

Uncle Murdoch strode over and squeezed Jeannie's shoulder. "She doesn't mean it," he mumbled. "She's just upset, of course." Jeannie nodded as if she understood completely.

Rev. Hope and Dr. Andrews helped Mama into the house, promising to stay through the night.

The Parker boys stayed the night, too. They'd come so far and wanted to start searching early, but insisted on sleeping in the barn loft. Jeannie pushed her fear and guilt into a corner for a while, concentrating on making them welcome. She brought blankets to lay over the hay. "We don't want to make work for you," Cap's oldest brother, Alf, said. He finally gave in when Jeannie just stood there, holding the blankets out. "You're as stubborn as Cap, Jeannie Shaw," he informed her.

The boys refused to come into the house because their boots and clothes were dirty, they said. They ate small portions when she served up the chicken stew. She didn't have brothers, but Jeannie had seen what Cap could eat at the Church Supper. She brought the remaining stew and a whole rhubarb pie to them after everyone else had finished.

"We need help using it up," she told them. "It won't keep."

When they finished, Tam spoke up. "Thanks for the supper, Jeannie. It was really good." The older brothers thanked her politely, too, and took the blankets up to prepare for the night.

Jeannie couldn't help smiling.

"What?" demanded Cap. "Do I have food on my chin, or something?"

"It's your manners, all of you," she said. "Pretty good . . . for boys."

Cap's face filled with amazement. "That's the nicest thing I've ever heard you say," he told her.

"I know," Jeannie admitted, looking at her feet. "I'm a bit sorry."

"I'll forgive you, though you don't deserve it. Ma says our problem is just that we're boys, but that she won't rest until we've learned to be gentlemen. She's gonna get awful tired first."

"My mother's the same; she says I have to learn not to be so 'righteous.'"

"Your mother's a smart lady."

She nodded. Cap nodded. They both grinned.

"So, I'll forgive you this time," he repeated.

"Though I don't deserve it?"

"Right."

"How's Essie?" she blurted, before she could chicken out.

"She's okay. Still not talking. But she let Mom trim her hair. It's real short now. Doesn't look too ugly, really."

161

"I'm sorry," Jeannie admitted. "I should have listened to you."

"Yes, you should have." He wasn't going to make it easy for her, she could see. He went on. "She asked Gran to take the cover off that sewing machine, you know. She hasn't done anything with it yet, just looks at it."

Jeannie felt a weight lift. In the midst of the search for Pearl and Ella, she hadn't realized it was still there, this worry over Essie.

"Here," Cap offered, "I'll carry these dishes back for you. That would be good manners, wouldn't it?"

They walked to the house. The lantern glow at the barn door reached toward the answering light from the kitchen. At the top step, Jeannie held her hands out for the dishes. She was framed in light.

Cap looked up at her. "Your ribbon," he said. Jeannie reached a hand up. "I saw the strangest thing today," he continued. "Ribbons, hanging from bushes. I didn't know it was ribbon-hunting season already."

Jeannie laughed. Then pain flashed through her. "I can't believe I just did that, forgot what's happened!"

"Ma says we should laugh all we can. Was it you put those ribbons out there?"

"It's stupid, I know," Jeannie told him. "I thought, what if the girls saw a ribbon, then another? I don't know, seems silly now. Anyway, I'd better get in and help clean up." She took the dishes from him.

"Jeannie? Tying ribbons on the bushes . . . it wasn't a bad idea. Really. My brothers and I do it all the time when we're in the woods – mark a trail by notching trees, I mean. A smart thing to do."

Jeannie nodded. "Thanks for telling me that. Good night, Cap."

Dr. Andrews came downstairs as Jeannie dried the last plates and put them on the shelf. "Your mother's resting," he said. "She wouldn't take anything except a little brandy in her tea. I'll check on her later. I gave your aunt something to help her sleep and got Murdoch to take her home."

Jeannie set a cup of tea on the table. Her hands shook at the reminder of her aunt and she was desperately glad not to have to face her again.

Rev. Hope came down soon after, shaking his head. "She's worn out, bless her. We'll both stay to offer what help we can."

"I could make up beds for you," Jeannie offered, "on the kitchen couch and in the living room."

"Don't trouble yourself, child," Dr. Andrews said. "We'll be fine. The reverend and I are used to all-night vigils. If there's any word," he added as he patted her shoulder, "we'll be sure to wake you."

Upstairs she tiptoed past her parents' room, where pale light shone under the door. Jeannie guessed at her mother lying awake, alone. Daddy had never been away overnight, except for the war. Constable Hennessy had questioned searchers, but only Mr. Phillips had met up with her father. Daddy had sent word to Mama that he was all right, shaken hands with Mr. Phillips, and disappeared back into the forest.

Jeannie retraced her steps and reached her hand out to her mother's doorknob. But she didn't touch it.

In her own room, she sat on a folded quilt at the window. The trees, black on black against the night, framed the dark hulk of barn. Blocks of lantern light shaped its doors and windows. Below her, spreading its glow beyond the veranda, a lamp was lit again in the porch.

"Good night, Pearl and Ella," Jeannie whispered. "Safe home." That's what Mama and Daddy always called when waving good-bye to visitors: "Safe home!"

When the lanterns were blown out in the barn, she got up from the window to lie on top of her bed. It was a comfort, she realized, having Cap and his brothers right across her yard. She had barely spoken all day. Words seemed too hard, too useless. Yet she had talked to Cap Parker, had even forgotten for a minute the awful reason he was here. It was the one bright spot in a horrible day. *Who'd have thought it? Cap, of all people.* She went over every word that had passed between them.

Jeannie would not have believed that sleep could possibly come. But it did. . . .

Before she even opened her eyes properly, Jeannie jumped up, anxious at seeing the sun so high, yet everything so quiet. She raced down, out the front door, and halted.

Mama sat in her rocker on the veranda, while Rev. Hope read softly from his Bible. The upper barn doors were flung open, showing the empty loft. *The boys've already gone, then. Everyone's gone. All these cars and trucks arrived, filled with people, and I didn't hear anything?*

Rev. Hope shut the Bible and said a prayer for Mama, his hand over hers. Mama's shoulders lifted in a deep breath, drawing the blessing in like necessary air.

Jeannie nodded to the minister. She leaned to kiss her mother's soft cheek. They smiled at her, but no one spoke. The silence was a relief.

Back in the kitchen, breakfast dishes were stacked by the sink, waiting to be washed. A note on the counter said, "Sorry to leave you with these, dear. I'm sure you won't mind. And I'm sorry for my words yesterday. I'm sure it wasn't your fault. I hope you'll forgive me. Love, Auntie Libby."

Jeannie smoothed the note over and over. It smelled of her aunt's lilac talcum powder. *How,* Jeannie wondered, *do you get from yesterday's words to these? Is this what Mama meant, that you have to forgive family?*

She picked up a dishcloth. Tears trickled one by one as if she were almost, but not quite, running out of them.

She kept busy all morning making endless sandwiches for those who came and went. Practically everyone who arrived brought food, too. She hated to see people carrying in the covered dishes, talking in hushed funereal tones.

Let them be found today. Let it be over.

At lunchtime Mama ate some soup for the sake of the baby. Her tea got cold beside her chair.

When a rifle shot shattered the afternoon air, everyone jumped. Within minutes, searchers hurried in from every direction, asking each other what was happening. Tina arrived with her fiancé. Auntie Libby and Uncle Murdoch returned together. Jeannie couldn't remember ever seeing them hold hands before.

Jeannie was afraid, too. 'Be careful what you wish for,' her mother would have said. She should have remembered that. She took it back – her wish for it to be over – tried to alter it. *What did that shot mean?*

It was another agonizing half hour before Cap Parker, rifle over his shoulder, came down the hill. A couple of dozen people waited silently. All you could hear was the scuff of Cap's boots as he crossed the yard. Mama stared down at her hands.

"Mrs. Shaw?" Cap began. "Found this by a stream, about an hour from here." He fumbled in his shirt. "Folks are checking that section now, and we want to spread word to head farther downstream. But we called to the girls for ages. We called and called."

He brought out a cup from inside his shirt. Mama reached for it. She turned it over, then nodded to her sister. The crowd parted. Auntie Libby sobbed and came to claim Ella's dented tin cup.

Uncle Murdoch walked up to Cap. "Thanks, son. We really appreciate...." He couldn't finish. He strode over to his dusty pickup truck and stood there with his back turned, one fist on the hood.

Rev. Hope climbed slowly up the steps and faced the crowd. "Friends and neighbors," he began, "let us pray. 'The Lord is my shepherd, I shall not want....'"

People took what comfort they could from the prayer, then returned to the search. Auntie Libby stayed with Mama while Uncle Murdoch left for the site where Ella's cup had been found. The sisters sat on the veranda and stared up at the hill meadow without talking. *What's left to say, after all?* Jeannie did not let herself turn away from their gray, sad faces. Punishing herself.

"Don't," Cap said, suddenly beside her. "Don't be so hard on yourself."

She sighed. "How hard should I be?" She kept watching the two mothers. "You know, even if Pearl and Ella turn up right this minute, it won't make it all better. Not *all* better, I know that!" She faced Cap. "When I was little, I broke my mother's one special ornament, her *Dancing Lady*. She got Daddy to glue it; said it was good as new.

But I know exactly where the crack is," Jeannie poked the air for emphasis, "and it will . . . always . . . be there! So don't tell me how to feel. Just tell me, Cap Parker, how would you feel?"

He didn't try to argue. Jeannie was too weary for this anger, anyway. "Mama wants me to lay out some lunch," she said. "You better come get some before you leave again."

From the cool cellar, they brought up platters of sliced ham and baked chicken, bowls of potato salad, and a pan of Mrs. MacDonald's date squares. They were about to serve themselves when the screen door banged open and three boys tumbled into the porch – John Angus, his younger brother Dan Archie, and the other boy from their class, Dougald MacFarlane.

John Angus leaned a long walking stick against the wall, among the hanging jackets. Its bark was freshly peeled. "Hi, Cap," he said. "Hi, Jeannie. Your mother sent us in to get something to eat. We're starving!"

"I'll get plates," she said.

The boys picked up ham slices, licked their fingers, then piled chicken and salad on, too. They pushed food onto their forks with their thumbs.

Jeannie bit her lip and caught Cap's eye, then looked away. *I guess if they were to find Pearl and Ella, I'd forgive their bad manners real quick.* She wished they'd hurry up and leave, though, before their noise made her scream. Finally, they pushed themselves away from the table, burping and groaning like old men. John Angus reached for the walking stick, still leaning against the wall in the porch.

Jeannie blinked and looked at him hard. "John Angus!" she called.

"Oh, yeah," he said. "Forgot my manners. Thanks for the food, Jeannie. See ya."

"Wait!" she shouted. "Where did you get those?"

"What? Get what?" John Angus looked all around.

"Those ribbons," she insisted. "On that stick! Where did you find them? I need to know!"

John Angus held the stick away to look at the several ribbons dangling from the top of it. "Oh, these? Found 'em in the woods, but a long ways from here."

Jeannie's eyes widened. "How many did you take?" she demanded.

John Angus squirmed, as if he'd been caught stealing cookies. "I don't know. Not many. Well, a few. I found them on bushes by the stream, followed them for a while, then heard these guys and headed off along the side trail. I didn't mean no harm!" he said, looking from her to Cap.

"Jeannie," Mama said, from the other side of the screen door. "What's this about? Why are these ribbons so important?"

"I left them there. To mark the trail for Pearl and Ella!" She wanted to scream in John Angus's face, but said it quietly, "Give them back."

John Angus tugged at the ribbons and sheepishly handed them over. "I'm awful sorry," he mumbled. "I didn't think. . . ."

"Yes," she agreed, "that's true." She cradled the strands in her shaking hands and left the kitchen.

Her mother found her sitting on the stairs, bent double as if in pain. Mama eased herself down beside her without speaking.

"He had no right!" Jeannie finally said, rocking back and forth. "I thought the girls might see them. I hoped they'd see them and know to follow them home."

She jumped up and headed for the porch. The kitchen was empty now.

"Where are you going?" Mama asked, following her out.

"I'm putting these back where I had them."

A gasp came from Mama. Then her voice hardened. "No! It's too far. I can't let you. With Pearl and Ella lost, and your father gone, too? It's too much!"

"Mama, please! I was there before."

"NO!"

"I'm sorry, Mama, I shouldn't ask, but –"

"Then don't ask it!"

Cap spoke from the veranda. "I could go with her, Mrs. Shaw. If Jeannie wants me to."

Jeannie and Mama looked at him, then at each other. Cap hurried on. "I know exactly where she has to go. John Angus told me. We'd be back by dark. If Jeannie'll let me go with her."

Jeannie stared at him. She finally nodded.

Mama took Jeannie's hand, still shaking her head, but "Go on, then," she said.

"Oh, thank you, Mama! Thank you, Cap," she said. "It means the world to me."

"That's all right," Cap replied awkwardly. "You need to change into pants and boots, though. And bring a jacket, even if it's warm right now."

"I'll fix some food for you to take," Mama offered. "Don't dawdle, Jeannie. Go change." Jeannie ran.

Back in the porch, she lifted her father's red plaid hunting jacket down from a peg. Mama emerged from the pantry with food tied in a dish towel. "Here. Now get a move on before I change my mind."

Jeannie hugged her. "Love you, Mama."

"I love you, too. Safe home, dear. You, too, Cap."

They ran all the way to the stream, then settled to a walk on the narrow trail. They spoke only to warn each other of branches or tree roots. Unseen searchers called Pearl's and Ella's names. Each call tore at Jeannie.

She shook her head as they passed the ribbons. Her bits of color, drooping from branches, seemed pathetic now – no better than needles in the haystack of this giant forest.

After an hour, Cap said, "There's a spot I know, coming up soon. We'll stop for a rest."

The stone slab, when they came to it, was as big as a tabletop and sloped into the stream. At normal water levels, most of its flat surface would have been submerged. Now it lay exposed.

"It's deeper off the end, there," Cap told her. "My father fished here a lot." It was all that was said before they went on. Jeannie didn't know what to say, anyway. One moment she was cross at Cap. The next, grateful.

She followed his back as he moved smoothly through the forest, already at home here. He held a branch aside so it wouldn't strike her.

"What are you grinning at?" she demanded.

He pointed to her clothes. "You could be my twin."

Jeannie grinned, too. Cap's jacket was the match of her father's. Most of the men and boys had the same one, all bought at Campbell's Store.

Their silence was more comfortable when they continued. As they passed another marker, Jeannie called, "I think we're almost there. These are tattered, like the ones John Angus took. I started using them when I ran out of everything else."

Finally, they passed a ribbon with no more ahead of it. "This is it," Jeannie declared. "This is where the ribbons are supposed to be."

It was late afternoon before they were done replacing the ribbons. Jeannie was reluctant to end their efforts and Cap agreed they could continue along her marked trail. When they realized they hadn't heard any other searchers for a while, they began calling out to the girls again.

After the final bit of ragged ribbon, Jeannie stood at the next bend and stared up the trail. She tugged the very last ribbon from her hair, tied it to a branch, and fashioned it into a perfect bow.

"Jeannie?" Cap's voice came to her as if from a great distance, but there he was, right beside her. "It'd be awful silly to carry this food all the way back. There's a deep spot just on a bit. It's always cooler there."

"Do you know every corner of these woods already?" she asked as they perched on a fallen log above the pool. "Here, have a sandwich. And an apple." She kept unwrapping food. "And some biscuits. And ham. And cookies. Mama must've put the whole pantry in here!"

They shared it out. Jeannie bit into a soft molasses cookie. "These are Pearl's favorites." She chewed for a while. "Cap, what if they're never found? Or it's too late?"

"*Aw*, Jeannie, don't –"

"Don't tell me don't! I was supposed to be looking after them, and now they might die out here. We might really lose them. You don't know what that's like!"

Cap went still as stone.

"Oh, Cap," she sighed, realizing what she'd said to the boy who'd lost his father. "I'm so stupid."

"It's okay."

"No, it's not. It's like Mama says. I'm too righteous. And I always blurt stuff out without thinking."

He didn't disagree. They finished their picnic in the forest quiet.

It was refreshing where they sat, above the dark salmon pool, away from the humid heat. A trickle of mountain water still swirled into the pool and wafted cooler air up to them.

"This is a good place," Cap said, looking up at the tops of the spruce trees, where they barely rocked in the breeze. "The weather's been warm, and there's lots of people looking for the girls. They really do have a chance, I promise."

Jeannie nodded. "Why did you offer to come with me?" she asked after a while. "It's not like I've been very nice."

He shrugged. "You asked how I'd feel if I were you."

"And?"

"I think I'd feel . . . alone."

Jeannie nodded again and stared into the pool. She couldn't speak without crying. And she'd cried so much already. Cap made it sound possible that the girls would be found. She held on to that and felt lighter.

He glanced up again. "Must be later than I thought." He started back along the log. "We'd better get moving."

"You're the boss . . . Crispus." She couldn't believe she'd said it.

Cap toppled off the log, but landed lightly. Jeannie kept her eyes on her feet as she walked the length of the log, then sat on the end of it.

"You know," Cap said, "you're not very nice." But he was smiling.

"It's true," she said. "I'm not. I'm only bringing it up now – Crispus – to tell you I'm sorry if you're embarrassed about your name – Crispus Aldershot, I mean."

"Will you stop saying that? Do you know how hard I have to work to hide that stupid name? You were right the first time, you know. I guess Mr. Moss felt sorry for me 'cause Essie's wasn't the only name he agreed to keep quiet."

"Why?" she asked. "Wouldn't it be better to get it over with? It's only a matter of time before someone gets hold of it."

"Someone already did!"

"Oh. Yes. Just don't make me cross, or watch out, Crispus! Anyway, I don't know how a mother looks into a cradle and says, 'He's my sweet wittle Crispus, yes he is!'"

"You think mine's bad? I was lucky. If you only knew some of the other names in our family."

She hopped down. "Really? What are they?"

"I can't. We promised each other we wouldn't tell. Come on, it's getting pretty dark."

Jeannie stomped along behind him. "That's not fair! You have to tell me now."

"Nope," he said over his shoulder. "Don't have to if I don't want to."

"You do, too! I'll tell Verity Campbell if you don't. Once she finds out, she'll blab it over the whole valley."

Cap stopped and turned slowly around. "No," he said. "I don't believe you. You're too nice." He started walking again.

"I am not! You said so, yourself."

"Yes, you are."

They argued their way along the trail. It was such a relief, it occurred to Jeannie, to be silly just for a little while.

By the time they got to the flat rock where they'd stopped on the outward journey, dusk had fallen. Cap checked the sky again when they stepped out onto the rock.

The water moved along with barely a sound. Even the breeze had stopped sighing through the treetops. "It's so quiet," Jeannie whispered, not wanting to spoil the peace.

"I come here a lot," Cap told her, "not just for fishing."

"Is this your Thinking Rock?" she asked.

"What? No, I just like it here."

"You must think while you're here, even if you are a boy. It's okay. I have a favorite rock, too," she admitted, "near our place."

"You just go there and think?" he asked.

"So?"

"I don't know" was all he said as he studied her.

They walked silently for a while, until Cap volunteered over his shoulder, "My oldest brother, Alf? He lets people think his name is Alfred, like our dad. It's really Aloysius Leesock Faradock. *A, L, F.* Alf."

Jeannie walked behind him without saying a word, but she pressed her lips together hard.

Cap kept going. "My cousin Essie. Her family's just as bad. Her name is Esther Serilla. And Moira's second name is Euphemia. When I want to make her mad, I call her Feemie."

Jeannie started to sputter.

Now Cap stopped on the path. Without turning, he began, "Paul's is the worst –"

"Stop!" Jeannie gasped. "How could it be worse?" She

grabbed a sapling for support and bent over with her other hand on her knee. "You're making these up!"

"They're too awful to be made up." He walked back and stood right in front of her, his hands in his jacket pockets. With a serious face, he continued. "Paul's is really Policarp –"

"No!"

"Ethelbert –"

"If I laugh any harder," Jeannie protested, "I'll have to go to the toilet!"

"Theophilus. See, he didn't use his initials like Alf and I did, or we'd've had to call him Pet. Pet wouldn't be much better as a name, he reckoned." Cap remained straight-faced, nodding while Jeannie laughed. "Guess I'll tell you the rest some other time," he ended.

When she got her breath back, she had to ask, "How could parents be so cruel?"

"Ma and her sister have a weakness for fancy names. They tell us we'll grow into them, whatever that means, and that we'll thank them someday. Most of them are 'fine honest Scots' names,' she says. I don't know about Policarp. It was Granddad's. Dan P., he was always called. No wonder."

Jeannie's laughter echoed through the woods.

"Okay, quit it," Cap ordered. "We gotta get going. Is it ever getting dark!"

They resumed their march, while Jeannie wiped her eyes with the cuff of her father's hunting jacket. Every now and then, she'd snicker again. Cap whistled the whole way.

They slowed their pace to keep from tripping on tree roots in the deepening gloom. When Cap stopped, Jeannie bumped right into him. "Sorry," she said. "Why'd you stop?"

"We're back."

"I see where we are now," she said. "Come on. It'll just take a sec." She pushed through underbrush. "See? This is my Thinking Rock." She felt along the side of the huge boulder, swung a foot into a notch, and was atop in an instant.

Cap craned his neck back. "Pretty good," he said.

She looked at him standing there. "Would you like to sit here, too?" she asked.

"Sure. *Uh,* how'd you get up there?"

"I thought you were supposed to be the forest expert."

"I'm a woodsman, not a rock climber."

"Here," she directed. "It's easy. Feel the ledges? Put one foot there, and the other here. That's right. There's even a seat for you."

They perched on the rock and listened to the small sounds of the stream. Jeannie spoke softly. "I won't tell anyone those names."

"Thanks."

"They're too awful."

"Sure are."

"They're the worst names –"

"All right, Jeannie Shaw!"

"Sorry." She became thoughtful. "The other day, when you saw me in the classroom, you knew I'd been sneaking into Mousie's desk and the register, didn't you?"

"Yep. Saw you through the window."

"But . . . you didn't tell on me."

"No. Maybe if you ever blab about my stupid name, I'll suddenly remember you're a burglar. But you won't tell."

"No. I promise."

"That's all right, then." He looked to the sky for the hundredth time. "I've been wondering why it got dark so darn early. Here, we've been worrying about a forest fire and instead we're gonna get a storm, looks like. Those are rain clouds. Big ones." He dropped down off the rock. "C'mon, Jeannie, we gotta go. Now!"

15

A tremendous flash of lightning lit the forest. Jeannie could see Cap as clear as day as he pulled on her arm. Whatever he was saying was lost in an angry clap of thunder. She ducked as if she'd been struck. They stumbled along the home path, blinded now by darkness, now by light. A clean wind came to meet them. Jeannie lifted her face to it, but hurried on.

The first raindrops hit as they followed the path from the stream up to the barn. They stepped out from under the trees and there was only the open yard now but, by the time they reached the house, the rain had become a deluge and they were drenched.

From the veranda, they watched searchers run in from all directions to shelter in the barn. Someone lit a lantern. Others pushed the big doors almost closed against the driving sheets of water. The rain drowned even the lantern light and Jeannie stopped counting how many had arrived. Her father was not among them.

"There won't be anyone searching now, will there?" she asked, but Cap didn't give her an answer. She knew, anyway. *To be out in the forest while such a storm fell. To be four years old, alone, and lost in this!*

The guilty weight came crashing down on Jeannie, all the heavier for stealing a carefree hour away. She tried to block the horrible pictures in her mind, but they came like the lightning. She could feel a scream rise in her, dark and wild. No one heard it over the long growl of thunder, not even Jeannie herself. But Cap saw it.

The door opened and Mrs. Campbell peered out. She waved them into the porch. "Oh, thank the Lord!" she cried over the storm. "Here they are at last. Get in here, child, so your poor mother can see you. You, too, Cap!"

A towel was draped over Jeannie as she was guided from one person to another through the crowded kitchen and presented like a prize to her mother, huddled in a chair by the stove. Jeannie dropped to her knees, laid her wet head in her mother's lap, and cried. Mama laid her own head down on her daughter's.

After a time, Dr. Andrews eased Jeannie up onto the couch and had Mrs. Campbell heat a cup of warm milk. "Drink it up," he said.

Friends and neighbors made quiet farewells and disappeared into the night while there was a lull in the storm. The doctor and Rev. Hope remained.

Mrs. Campbell put a bowl of soup in front of Cap and laid a quilt over Jeannie. After he ate, Cap got up to speak to Mrs. Campbell. She fished in her purse and handed him a pencil and a used envelope to write on. He returned to the table. Jeannie saw him look over at her, then he started to write.

Mrs. Campbell tied a scarf on her head and waited at the door for her husband to pick her up. Cap took his finished note to her. He asked her something Jeannie couldn't hear. Mrs. Campbell exclaimed, "You dear boy," and patted his cheek. A truck horn beeped and she hurried out.

Cap thanked Mama for the soup. She smiled at him. At the door, he looked back to Jeannie, curled up in a corner of the couch. She managed a twitch of her mouth that could barely be called a smile. Cap waved to her and left for the barn and his brothers.

Dr. Andrews ordered Jeannie off to bed. At the foot of the stairs, he said, "Jeannie, I'd like you to stay close to your mother tomorrow." He cut off her feeble protest. "She's worried sick, and I mean that as her doctor. No going off and scaring her half to death again, you hear?"

Jeannie dragged herself up to her room, dropped

jacket and socks on the floor. She blew out the lamp and lay down fully clothed, too weary for more effort, then groped in the dark until she felt her father's hunting jacket again. It was almost dry. She pulled it in beside her, sniffed its pipe and pine smell, and kept it there. Lightning flashed and thunder snarled.

The storm fought on all night. Jeannie didn't hear it....

The wild weather had died away by dawn. Jeannie opened her puffy eyes and pushed back her father's jacket. Moving in slow motion, she took off her wrinkled blouse, stepped out of the mud-spattered pants, and slipped into the first dress that came to hand. It was the new one, with blue and pink forget-me-nots.

She brushed her matted hair a bit, but had nothing left now to tie it back. It flopped in her face, still half tangled. It didn't matter. She set the brush down. Nothing mattered.

Her feet on the stairs made no sound. The hall clock showed it was just past six as she stood in the kitchen doorway. She felt almost invisible, like mist.

Dr. Andrews and Rev. Hope were drinking tea at the table. Rev. Hope nodded and shook his head in turns, as the doctor was saying, "... danger of flash floods now, they say. The runoff after that rain is something awful! We can only hope those little girls keep well away from –"

He stopped when he noticed Jeannie in the doorway. "Oh. Good morning, Jeannie. Don't you look nice."

Jeannie drifted right past them with hardly a nod, and out the door to look at the day. The sky was pale gray and the merest mizzle of rain still fell. Some searchers had already started out.

Mr. Phillips and the Campbells drove in at the same time. They got out and talked quietly, shaking their heads. The barn doors pushed back. Cap and his brothers emerged, stretching, rubbing their eyes. Their hair lay in sleepy clumps, and bits of hay stuck to them.

Mama and Auntie Libby stepped out of the vegetable garden and bent to lift a bucket of potatoes between them. Jeannie had never noticed before how closely they resembled each other. *Do Pearl and I look that much alike?*

Mr. Phillips and Mr. Campbell hurried forward to carry the pail of potatoes. Mrs. Campbell picked her way around the puddles in the yard and handed Alf a bulky paper bag. She gave Cap a piece of paper and a small packet. Cap looked at the paper, then stuffed it and the package into his pocket.

Mrs. Campbell went to join Mama and Auntie Libby, giving them each a quick hug. How large and hearty the storekeeper looked beside the small frames of the sisters, even with Mama's pregnancy rounding out her dress.

Jeannie marveled at how perfectly peaceful the

morning looked. *It must be like this every day for Essie: something falling apart, but the world keeps right on spinning while you suffer.*

What will happen today? she wondered. *This has to be over soon . . . one way or another. Surely they'll be found.* But life wasn't like that. Troubles, she knew, didn't always sort themselves out like the plots of books, otherwise fathers would come home safely from war, polio would go away like measles, and everyone would live happily ever after.

Mama smiled up at her from the bottom step. "You did a lovely job making that dress, dear," she said.

"How do you keep going, Mama?" Jeannie asked. "How do you do it?"

Mama came up the steps. "One foot in front of the other, dear." She kissed her daughter's head and went in. Jeannie followed.

The Parker boys ate a hurried breakfast. Cap stayed behind when his brothers went to get ready. "Can I talk to you, Jeannie?" he asked.

She put down the dish towel. "Sure."

"The Campbells took a message to Mom for us last night," he said. "We needed clean socks and stuff. Anyway, there's two things I want to tell you. I wrote a note telling Essie you were asking about her." He pulled the paper out of his pocket. "Essie sent you this."

Dear Jeannie,

I'm sad to hear that your sister and cousin are missing. It must be awful for you. Don't give up. I'll be thinking of you. Essie.

P.S. I read your letter. I'll forgive you if you'll forgive me. When the girls are found, I hope you'll visit me again.

P.P.S. I guess I forgot that other people have troubles, too.

"Pretty good, huh?" asked Cap.

Jeannie nodded. It was good. She and Cap were getting along, and now it looked like she would get to know Essie after all. Two new friends. It was more than she'd ever wished for.

I'd give them both up in a blink, if I could just have Pearl and Ella back.

"Thank you for this," she told Cap. "Did you say there was something else?"

Cap's face went red. *It's not bad,* Jeannie decided, *having someone around who blushes as much as I do.*

"Well . . . ," he began. "Okay. See, I got Mrs. Campbell to bring these from her store for me. For you, I mean!" He brought out the crumpled paper packet. "I suppose they're messed up now, but, well, when I saw you'd given up all your ribbons like that. . . . Here, these are for you."

He thrust the package at her like it was too hot. Jeannie held it, finally opened it. Inside were two wide velvet ribbons – the best quality from Campbell's Store – one white, one a soft blue. Not pale blue, not dark – blueberry blue.

"Oh, Cap," she said. "Why? I mean, you shouldn't have."

"Well, I did. Anyway, your hair was getting messy."

She smiled. "Gee, thanks."

"What are friends for?"

She ran the ribbons through her fingers and looked at him. "You're not the friend I imagined," she said. "No! I didn't mean it like that. I'd really like us to be friends. You're easy to talk to . . . when you're not insulting me."

"Same here," he said, relaxing. "Well, anyway. I better get going before my brothers start yelling at me some more."

"Thanks, Cap."

"That's all right."

She went to the door and watched the brothers set off. *I have a friend,* she thought, *and his name is Cap.*

As she wiped the table and swept the floor, she thought, *I have a friend.*

She drifted upstairs, touching the ribbons in her pocket. She brushed her hair properly and tied the blue velvet ribbon in her curls. The other ribbon she laid on the dresser, smoothing it out.

"I have a friend," she announced aloud, for the first time, to her reflection.

When a shaft of sunlight glinted in the mirror, Jeannie knelt at her window. The day was turning sharp and clear, the sun poking through. The grass was green again, the bushes and trees were washed.

Barncat lapped at a puddle in the yard. A water paddler bug landed on the surface and Barncat jumped back, smack into another puddle. He jumped sideways out of that one. He shook each paw in turn.

"Pearl," Jeannie murmured, "come home and see this. You'll laugh and laugh."

She looked to the hill. *If I stare hard enough, Pearl and Ella will appear. They just have to!* She stared until her eyes watered, until she could see nothing at all.

Downstairs again, the only people around were Mama and Rev. Hope, sitting silently on the veranda. Mama had barely spoken for days, Jeannie realized. Not a scrap of poem, a line of song, not even the Bible.

Everyone else had gone off in another big search effort. *How long before they have to give up?* Jeannie wondered. She knew she would shatter the first time anyone dared utter the thought aloud.

Barn, house, and yard soon dried. The rosebushes rustled in a breeze, each leaf standing out sharp-edged in the washed air. There was not one unfamiliar detail, but it all looked unreal to her. Jeannie settled on the step where Lady should be. The quiet world waited. The sun moved carefully across the morning. . . .

A shot blasted in the distance. Birds rose into the air like solid echoes. Jeannie searched the horizon in panic, as if the reason for the shot should appear immediately. She searched for the answer in her mother's face.

How small Mama seemed, wrapped in a thick shawl, even in this heat. Her knuckles were white as they gripped the rocker. Rev. Hope opened his Bible again. "I will lift up mine eyes unto the hills," he read, "from whence cometh my help."

People returned and asked each other what it could mean this time. Cap and his brother Paul showed up, but neither of them had fired the shot.

"Jeannie?" Cap asked, but she couldn't seem to break the trance that was holding her taut. A corner of her mind watched herself. *Here I am, waiting to stop waiting. Here is Mama. Here is Cap. So this is how the world shifts from under you.*

The searchers gathered into an ever tighter, protective circle. Their voices dwindled to church-sized murmurs, trying not to hope too much, trying not to give up hoping.

Jeannie stood on tiptoe to see over their heads. She strained to hear over their voices. *What was that?* It came again – the rough, gruff *woof* of a dog.

"Lady?" Jeannie tried to call.

Everyone turned to look at Jeannie, questioning her. And, so, she alone saw the new cluster of searchers appear in a rush around the far corner of the barn. Alf Parker led them. And Lady, limping but lively, led him.

"Mama," Jeannie said. It came out no louder than breath, a child's cry on the edge of nightmare. "Mama!" she managed.

Mama looked up and started to rise. Rev. Hope grasped her arm to steady her. His lips moved in speeded-up prayer.

Jeannie swung her head back so she wouldn't miss anything, and yet was afraid to face whatever was coming. Everyone in the yard turned now, too.

The approaching crowd parted, revealing Jeannie's father carrying in his wiry arms the two little girls, limp and still against his shoulders.

Jeannie's heart froze. "Move," she whispered, but whether to herself or the two children, she didn't know.

Pearl lifted her head from Daddy's shoulder. She had her tin cup hooked in her finger.

Jeannie still couldn't move, not until Mama came

rushing past and grabbed her hand, so that they flew together to the center of the circle.

Ella lifted her head, too. Both Jeannie and Mama cried out at the sight of them. They had so many scratches and mosquito bites, the cousins looked like they'd gotten chicken pox together all over again.

"Mama!" Pearl called, reaching out. Mama hugged her fiercely with one arm, not letting go of Jeannie with the other. Pearl finally protested, "You're squishing me, Mama!" And they could all laugh at last, all but Jeannie. Mama let go of Pearl long enough to give Ella a squeeze and a kiss, too.

Uncle Murdoch came tearing down the hill, more scratched than the girls from fighting his long way back through the forest since he'd heard the shot. He scooped Ella into his arms and shook hands with Daddy all at the same time.

Daddy, dark-chinned from not shaving, dark circles under his eyes from not sleeping, spoke to the smiling crowd, but most of the time he looked at Pearl. "Found them by a waterfall," he said. "Far down the valley. Farther than any of us were searching! They just keep saying they walked and walked, thinking they'd get home."

Jeannie stood there in the middle of it all. She saw it unfolding like the pages of a book. *What if I'm still sitting on the step waiting,* she wondered, *making this up in my head like I always do, just wishing it?* She was afraid to blink in case it disappeared, in case it wasn't true. *And if it is true, will Pearl ever forgive me? Mama says that's what families do.*

"It was Lady who found them," Daddy told everyone. "She showed up yesterday afternoon, but it was too far to bring her home. Good thing! Round about supper, she caught a scent, then lost it at the waterfall. I tried to get her to come away, but she wouldn't quit the place." Daddy crouched and scratched behind Lady's ears. "Kept sniffing around some kind of twig house. When I saw it was put together on purpose, I came back and searched every corner. The girls waded through the water again – that's why Lady lost their scent – and hid under a rock overhang, keeping out of that storm. The waterfall was so loud we couldn't have heard each other if we tried. There they were, asleep on pine needles. Pretty weak, I'll tell ya. Darn lucky the rock shelf was above the water when it rose last night! You found them, didn't you, Lady? You found Pearl and Ella!"

When she heard Pearl's name, Lady perked up her head. People were reaching to pat the dog from all directions.

" 'Seek and ye shall find,' " Mama said as she patted Lady, too. "Good girl. Best old girl in all the world!"

"But it was the queer little twig houses they made,"

Daddy went on. "If not for those, Lady and I would've never known to keep looking. Never known!"

Pearl clapped her hand over her father's mouth before he could say more. "Jeannie did it!" she declared. "Jeannie showed us how to make the fairy houses."

Everyone started patting Jeannie on the back. She felt like Lady when they did, but she smiled at last when she felt Mama squeeze her hand and let go.

Daddy kissed Jeannie's forehead, then went back to staring at his Pearl. Mama stood up slowly and lifted her hand to her husband's bristled cheek. She touched his hair.

As a last cloud drifted away, Jeannie tried to take in all the details, to make sure it was real. Sun shone on them gathered there, shone on the house and barn, shone on the dangerous dark emerald forest and softened it again to leaf and moss and meadow greens, all dappled and gentle in the clean air.

Jeannie watched her mother shade her eyes to look at Daddy. *What does Mama see?* The sun showed what they'd missed so far. All through her father's dark hair, shocks of silver gray had appeared. Three days ago, he'd had no gray hair at all. Mama rested her head against his shoulder.

Constable Hennessy's car careered up the drive, blaring its horn. He had raced to get Auntie Libby, who had been resting at home. She jumped from the car now amid a cheer from the crowd and ran into her husband's arms, laughing, sobbing, and clutching her Ella.

"Mommy," Ella mumbled into her mother's neck.

"Look, Jeannie." Pearl held a grubby fist under her sister's nose. "We picked ribbons from the bushes. That's better than blueberries!"

Everyone hushed to listen. Pearl was in her glory now. "We didn't know where to go for a long, long time. We tried to go through the woods, but it was too hard. And it was scarier than any old ghost!"

Ella chimed in. "I was afraid the Bochdan would get us, but Pearl says there's no such thing."

Pearl wanted the attention back on her. "We found the water again and I saw a ribbon, then Ella saw one. We kept picking ribbons, but we didn't ever get home. Then the bad rain came. Then Lady and Daddy! We picked these all the way back. They're for you, Jeannie!"

Jeannie stared at the tangle of ribbons and lace in Pearl's fist. "No, Pearl, you can have them for playing with. I'll help you clean them up good as new."

Pearl's tangled hair hung in her face. Jeannie plucked pine needles and shreds of moss from it. She slid the new ribbon from her own hair. "Here," she said, "let's make you pretty again." Daddy leaned forward so Jeannie could reach.

Pearl held onto Jeannie's hand and examined the

blueberry blue velvet ribbon. "This is fancy," she said. "It's awful pretty. Is it your birthday present?"

Jeannie gave a surprised laugh.

Mama counted on her fingers and cried, "She's right! It's your birthday, Jeannie. Oh, I'm so sorry."

"That's all right, Mama," Jeannie said. "Even I forgot, honest." She couldn't get over it. "I'm twelve!"

"But who gave you a birthday present," Pearl demanded, "if everyone forgot?"

Jeannie searched the crowd until she saw him. "Cap," she told Pearl. "My friend, Cap, gave it to me."

"Hi, pip-squeak!" Pearl called to Cap. She laughed and laughed at her joke.

Cap came forward. "Pip-squeak, yourself," he said. "We sure are glad to see you two." He tapped Jeannie's shoulder. "Is it really your birthday?"

"I guess so."

"Then those ribbons are your birthday present. Wasn't I smart? Happy birthday, Jeannie."

"Well," proclaimed Mama, "I have a cake to bake, don't I?" But Mrs. MacDonald declared she wanted to make it, the biggest cake the valley had ever seen. Mrs. Campbell hurried off to make lemonade, and to bring Lady a whole bag of beef bones as a reward, she told them.

Lady made her way up the steps. She turned herself around, plopped down in her favorite spot, and barked once. She watched everyone rushing around, then fell asleep.

Cap and his brothers went to the barn to get cleaned up. Rev. Hope and Father MacNeil left to fetch their fiddles. Verity called out from her parents' car, "We're going to pick something nice for your birthday!" Sarah and Melanie leaned out the same window and waved, too.

Jeannie grinned as she waved to them. *If they only knew how much they look like the Three-Headed Monster right now.*

We're going to have a party, she realized, *and everyone's going to be here, even Verity Campbell. There's never been anyone but family at my birthday before. I'll wear my new shoes. I wish Essie could come.*

She let the wish go as soon as it arrived. *No more wishes,* she lectured herself. She'd write Essie another note, though, and maybe send a piece of that birthday cake. But it wasn't time for Essie Phalen to come visiting yet.

Tina and her Edwin, in another crowd of returning searchers, rushed past to help celebrate the good news. Tina's eyes met Jeannie's accidentally and, as quickly, she looked away.

This'll take time to mend, too, Jeannie figured. Maybe the crack would always be there. She'd have to live with it. Another thing to think about at her rock later. But, first, the party.

"I know!" she said aloud and hurried over to the doctor's car.

"That's a great idea, Jeannie!" Dr. Andrews exclaimed. "I'll go get her right now." And he drove off to invite Cap's mother to bring her little niece, Moira, to the celebration.

Pearl and Ella will like that, Jeannie thought. *At least I'll have Cap here, and that's fine.*

Besides, she knew, the party would be more about the little girls being found than about Jeannie Shaw turning twelve. That was fine, too. Everything was fine . . . almost.

Jeannie tugged on her sister's hand and made the words come out. "I'm so sorry, Pearl."

"What for?"

"For losing you, of course."

"You didn't lose me, stupid! I lost me all by myself. Ella was scareder than I was, so I looked after her." She wiggled her grubby fingers at Ella, who waved back from her safe place between her parents.

"I'm still sorry," Jeannie insisted.

"Are you sorry enough," Pearl tried, "to let me wear your birthday ribbon anyway?"

"Sure. You're a birthday present, too, Pearl. You and Ella. Here, let's wrap up my big present. There you are," she said as she reached up at last and tied Cap's birthday present in her sister's hair.

"There you are," Jeannie said again.

ACKNOWLEDGMENTS

Thanks to Ella Ingraham and family, to Dougald MacFarlane, and to Jim St.Clair for answering my hundreds of questions about the area and the era.